The Heartbreak Club

Novoneel Chakraborty is the prolific author of 17 bestselling thrillers, one e-novella, one bestselling short story collection and one audio novel. His works have been translated into multiple Indian languages. Almost all his novels have debuted in the top three ranks in the Neilsen listings, in India.

His Forever Series made it to the *Time of India*'s 'Most Stunning Books of 2017', while the Stranger Trilogy became a phenomenal hit amongst young adults, with Amazon tagging it, along with his erotic thriller, *Black Suits You*, as their memorable reads of the year. Known for his solid plotting, unpredictable twists and strong female protagonists, he is also referred to as the 'Sidney Sheldon of India' by his readers.

His immensely popular thrillers—books in the Stranger Trilogy, the Forever Series and *Black Suits You*—have been adapted for screen. Apart from novels, Novoneel has written and developed several hit TV and original web shows for premiere channels like Mx Player, Sony, Star Plus, Zee and Zee5. He lives and works in Mumbai.

NOVONEEL CHAKRABORTY

The Heartbreak Club

First published by Westland Books, a division of Nasadiya Technologies Private Limited, in 2024

No. 269/2B, First Floor, 'Irai Arul', Vimalraj Street, Nethaji Nagar, Alapakkam Main Road, Maduravoyal, Chennai 600095

Westland and the Westland logo are the trademarks of Nasadiya Technologies Private Limited, or its affiliates.

Copyright © Novoneel Chakraborty, 2024

Novoneel Chakraborty asserts the moral right to be identified as the author of this work.

ISBN: 9789360454845

10 9 8 7 6 5 4 3 2 1

This is a work of fiction. Names, characters, organisations, places, events and incidents are either products of the author's imagination or used fictitiously.

All rights reserved

Typeset by R. Ajith Kumar, Delhi

Printed at Nutech Print Services, India

No part of this book may be reproduced, or stored in a retrieval system, or transmitted in any form or by any means, electronic, mechanical, photocopying, recording, or otherwise, without express written permission of the publisher.

For everyone who has lost something important in life

A WORD OF ADVICE

My loyal readers would vouch for the fact that even though I write thrillers, my stories often minutely explore man–woman relationships. And keeping in mind today's fast-changing times, I would like to point towards one relationship red flag. I read somewhere that people who claim to be in love, do two things. Either they pluck the flower they love or they water it daily, for it to blossom.

The quote stayed with me. I believe anyone who is trying to 'pluck' you, terminating your potential in the name of love, is someone from whom you have to stay away. It doesn't matter how intensely you feel for them. What I have come to understand in life, is that anything which terminates your own relationship with yourself, turning you into an unrecognisable alien, can never be love. The wisdom lies in knowing who is 'plucking' you and who is, 'watering' you. That is the essence of all relationships.

Be alert, be wise and be at peace.

With Love

PROLOGUE

43, Hawstead Road, Catford, London.

NOT MUCH HAD CHANGED IN THE HOUSE. THE BEAUTIFUL fiddle leaf fig she had planted some time back, now looked taller, there was a layer of dust on her book shelf and Fluff, her golden retriever, looked bigger than before. But other than that, the house looked the same.

It had been six months since Kisha Sen was taken to a rehabilitation centre after a shocking episode, where she lost her cool and hit a classmate on the head with a duster. Today, she had come back home. Rehabilitated, at least on paper. The anger issue, though, was nothing new for her.

At sixteen, Kisha Sen was already an achiever. She had won numerous awards for her role as a teen-environmentalist, thereby becoming a vehement voice in climate change activism. Her claim to fame was a series of tweets where she had formulated ten points, tagging various world leaders and organisations for prompt action on the climate crisis while suggesting some immediate measures. The trigger for her onward march to being taken seriously by the world happened when the offices of two senators in the UK retweeted her. Later in the year, Kisha was also given the opportunity to take part in the United Nations Climate Change Conference. Her twenty-minute lecture there went viral on social media and raised a storm amongst teens in various parts of the world.

In her school, Fairmont High International, she was a topper. Everything was going well, but before she could be declared the best student in the school for the year, her anger issues emerged. First, it was a one-off argument with the teacher, where she raised her pitch a little too much for comfort. Then, a while later, it was about pushing a girl after class who, according to Kisha, was getting on her nerves with her constant chatter. Then there was the incident of her throwing an angry fit in front of the principal because she wanted to be a part of an inter-school Olympiad but Fairmont High wasn't interested. Finally, it was the duster incident which convinced the authorities that Kisha needed some time off. Her worried parents consulted with the school therapists and it was decided she would be sent off for anger management therapy.

The rehab was designed as an extension of the school, so students who were sent there wouldn't miss their classes. It was more of a residential rehab which ran on the principles of discipline and monitoring with empathy. In the ensuing three months, Kisha didn't visit home. She had come to the centre with a resolve. She wanted to heal herself in a conscious way. What she did do there was read. She read books on child psychology, where it said that most of the times the negative emotions children express have either been subliminally absorbed by them as toddlers at home or are a response to some pent up emotions. It also said that most of what we are is because of the kind of parenting we get, and most of what we become is our own individual choice, however subconscious that may be. With all this in mind, Kisha knew exactly what she had to ask her mother when she met her at home, post rehab.

'What did you mean when you compared my anger problems to dad's?'

Her mother sighed. 'I hate to say this but you're a copy of him, Kish. He has a nasty temper, and you are just like him,' Ranya Sen said, spooning some salad into her mouth, as Kisha sat at the lunch table dumbfounded. The nonchalance didn't surprise her. She'd rarely found her mother moved by anything. It was as if she anticipated most things and had a response ready in her mind. Maybe she had known Kisha would pose this question at some point in time.

Kisha knew two things about her parents. When they all lived in London, her parents used to fight a lot but tried to pretend all was good in front of her and her elder sister, Anara. Then good sense prevailed and the two divorced a year ago. Anara went to India with her father, while Kisha and Ranya stayed back in London.

'How is Anara di doing?' Kisha asked to change the subject. She was in touch with Anara for the past three months that she had been in rehab but not thoroughly. Phones weren't allowed there. Nor was the internet. The rehab purposely didn't allow certain comforts. One of the reasons for that was that the authorities knew there were many smarty pants in the school who would feign behavioural issues just to stay in the rehab's safe environment from time to time. The rehab was there to provide an environment to detox for students who needed it. While Kisha was there it was only Ranya who would come down every fortnight to check on her. And that's when Kisha used to talk to her sister on video call. But from the past two months, that hadn't happened either. Every time Ranya went to the rehab and Kisha asked her to call up Anara, she said, 'Anara isn't keeping well. Talk to her when you are home.'

Ranya glanced at her, a tad unsure, then picked up her phone.

'We need to talk, Kish, but excuse me now. Work call.' Half done with her lunch, she went to the other room.

'Typical,' Kisha muttered under her breath.

The Sens had migrated from C.R. Park in New Delhi to the UK after Prithibi Sen married Ranya. He was an investment banker and when a suitable opportunity presented itself in the UK, he thought it would be good for his career as well as the kids he eventually wanted to have with his new wife. Also, he was done with his mother's over possessiveness of him. Prithibi and Ranya Sen flew to London to start a new life together. Both Anara and Kisha were born in the UK and were British citizens. In Delhi, Ranya, a trained chef, was a housewife for a year after her marriage, but in London she joined a famous restaurant as a sous chef. Though Ranya never confessed this to anyone, work was her pain-killer. Immersing herself in work, she realised, gave her less time to dwell on her sorrows of a broken marriage which had once looked promising.

With Ranya disappearing into her room, clearly desirous of avoiding conversation, Kisha too lifted her lunch plate and ambled to her room. She sat down by the study chair and spooned some of the scrambled eggs into her mouth while looking around. It used to be Anara's room till she shifted to India. Kisha had moved into it when Anara left; but before she could make it hers the rehab stint had happened. Looking at it now, Kisha wondered if the room was bigger than hers. Before going to the rehab centre, she'd turned her own room into a mini-nursery. This was an acquired interest she had taken on from Anara. Kisha went to the photo frames fixed above her study table. Most of the photographs were hers but there were five which were with Anara. Different times. Different moods. Kisha could recollect the story behind every click. And as she did, the smile kept stretching on her face. The third photograph in particular was clicked on the day when Kisha had her first stage elocution. She used to stammer when she was nervous, and she was scared she would mess up her performance. It was Anara who made her practice for days and nights till the performance happened. It turned out to be Kisha's first award as well. As Kisha caressed the photograph, she felt her eyes moistening. Anara had believed in her when she hadn't.

Kisha kept her plate on the study table. She picked up her phone and checked her WhatsApp. There was no response from Anara yet. Kisha had messaged her sister the moment she was back, earlier in the day: *Hey sis, how are you? I'm finally back home from rehab. Want to talk?* The single tick told her the message had not been received on Anara's phone. Kisha decided to go on Twitter next.

As the app loaded itself after three months, she felt relieved. It was a sign that her normal life was finally back. She looked through her many notifications. There were several new messages, many from her classmates and friends. The latest message was sent by an account with no profile picture. The sender's name read: anonymous1234345. Before Kisha could categorise the message as junk, her eyes fell on the first line of the message, visible even without opening it. Kisha tapped on the message and read it. Not once. But three times.

You think Anara disappeared just like that? Lol. No! The Heartbreak Club is responsible, li'l sis.

ONE

Six Months Later
Fairmont High International, Noida

NEVER IN HER WILDEST DREAMS HAD KISHA THOUGHT she would be 40,000 feet above the ground on her seventeenth birthday. That too all by herself. Sure, she had four other students of Fairmont High International, London, on the same flight to New Delhi, but they weren't from her section. As part of an annual exchange programme, five students, with overall ace results and in their penultimate year of passing school, were shuffled between the different branches of Fairmont High, world over. Five students from their California branch went to their Sydney branch and, in exchange, five students from their Sydney branch arrived at the California branch. Similarly, five from the London branch went to New Delhi (NCR) and vice versa.

Kisha was one of the five who was selected for the London–New Delhi (NCR) exchange. And it wasn't a random decision or any thrill of coming back to roots that had led her to apply for the exchange programme. The reason was rather simple: she wanted to know what had happened to her elder sister, Anara Sen. And what the hell was the Heartbreak Club, as mentioned in the anonymous Twitter message. Sitting by the window seat of the aircraft, Kisha wondered how good it would have been if the two sisters could relocate together.

Anara always had an inkling of what was brewing between her parents. And that a divorce was round the corner. And when it happened, her father shifted to Delhi with an entrepreneurial spirit and a blueprint of setting up a fintech startup while Ranya stayed in London with the girls. The divorce battle was initiated. The judge, seeing that both parents had equal financial standing, allowed them to have the custody of one daughter each, leaving the choice of parent to the daughters. Anara knew choosing her father meant choosing a different country, a different social set up and a different set of friends. She chose to be with Prithibi knowing well that Kisha wouldn't be able to adapt to so many things so soon.

Neither Anara nor Kisha really understood what had gone wrong with their parents' relationship. The seed of separation was sown by the common indifference which they both had developed towards each other. But when did the indifference surface and why? Both the daughters had heard a lot about the intense love story of their parents from relatives. But as they grew up, neither could see the intensity. Prithibi and Ranya seemed like two different people living together only because they had kids. That seemed to be the only glue binding them. And with time, that glue too lost its stickiness. Their fights kept increasing and the topics ranged from serious to trivial ones. Till a point came when they only spoke to fight. When they decided to separate, the children knew it was for the best.

Anara accompanied Prithibi to New Delhi. Fairmont High, New Delhi (NCR) was a residential school so Anara moved in to the school's girls' hostel on the sprawling campus, while Prithibi stayed in C.R.Park, in the house he had once grown up in. Both his parents were dead by now. A long-time caretaker and her family had been looking after the house. It had been eleven months and everything was going smoothly till suddenly Anara went missing. Disappeared into thin air.

Kisha was in rehab at the time and didn't find out, since her parents were worried about the effect it would have on her. It was also the reason why Ranya couldn't fly to India.

'Anything new from the police?' Kisha asked almost as soon as she met her father at the arrivals lounge of the New Delhi International Airport. From the time Kisha had read the anonymous message about Anara's disappearance, she had been in sheer disbelief. She had hounded her mother for the truth and finally Ranya had come clean.

'Your dad got a call from the school authorities one day, saying Anara was not to be found anywhere,' Ranya said and, a deep breath later, added, 'We did our best, involved the police, but she still hasn't been found.' Kisha felt as if someone had sucked all the air from her lungs and left a forever vacuum.

Ignoring her question, Prithibi gave her a smile and hugged her. He was overjoyed to see Kisha, and especially at the prospect that she would live in Noida for the next six months, as per the exchange program. He had been lost and miserable since Anara's disappearance. His loneliness and grief were evident in the way he hugged Kisha tight. And as he broke the embrace, she looked at his eyes and asked him the same thing again. This time, Prithibi couldn't dodge it.

'Nothing new. The police did their investigation well. They haven't closed the case but what they told me is that it's a school matter. They are juveniles after all.' He took a thoughtful pause, 'As I told you on the phone, let's not forget that they are all kids of the who's who of India. Police could squeeze out nothing from the students. And while the school did its best to cooperate with the police, it can't let the police be on campus forever. It would compromise their brand value. The investigation is still ongoing though. The officer told me they didn't get any leads. They can't figure out a motive for Anara to go missing. No ransom call came either,' Prithibi said, sounding disturbed.

'Isn't it weird that a girl goes missing from her school and nobody has a clue? And on top of it neither the police, nor the school can do anything?' Kisha said.

'Kish, everyone did their best. I know. I saw how the investigation was going. It's only after trying everything that they have sort of reached a conclusion.'

'What is the conclusion?' Kisha saw her father avert his eyes, as if he was in two minds whether to tell her or not. Seeing her staring at him expectantly for an answer, Prithibi knew he couldn't bypass this one, this time.

'Kish, they think Anara disappeared of her own accord.'

'What? That's bullshit.' *Why would Anara di do that? Where would she go?*

'That she was affected by your mother and my marital turmoil and her disappearance is her way of coping with the situation. Just like with you and your anger issues. Teens do these things, I'm told,' he continued.

'Did she show any signs of being troubled?'

Prithibi shook his head and said, 'Sometimes teens don't come out clean and retreat in to a shell instead.'

Even if Anara was affected she was not the kind to run away, Kisha thought. Her elder sister was a fighter. She loved to confront the situation and not find excuses to escape. In fact, it was Anara who had also taught Kisha to face situations in life, than turn one's back on them. So, to think of her disappearance as a defense mechanism was complete nonsense for Kisha. And if she would have done it, she would have been in touch with her at least.

'Whatever that's supposed to mean,' Kisha said aloud as the car swerved on the driveway leading up to the school. The drive was a silent one. Since the time Kisha had heard about Anara's disappearance, all the moments she spent with her kept coming back to her. Especially, the last time she saw her outside the Heathrow airport where Kisha had gone to see her off before she left for India with their dad.

'I don't know why they had to have two kids if this is what they wanted; a fucking divorce.'

'Language, Kish,' Anara had said patronisingly. 'Adulting is much tougher than "teenageing" is what I've understood.'

'That can't be an explanation for their divorce. Do they understand they are separating us as well?' Kisha was both angry and emotional.

'Oh Kish! Nobody can separate us, li'l one. And why, now you will have my room. You used to crib about your room all the time,' Anara had said with a laugh.

Kisha glanced at her elder sister, then leaped on to her, hugging her the way a baby hugs a parent when scared.

'I will miss you, di. Like seriously.'

'I'll miss you too, li'l one.' Anara's voice choked. 'But don't let all this trouble you. Whatever happens, happens for the best. And it's a matter of a year. I'll pass out from school and then come back here for my undergrad.'

Kisha's face lit up with a smile. 'Promise?'
'Pinky promise.' Anara had smiled.

The school, as she observed, while driving in with her father, was much bigger compared to her school in London. But she felt the building had no charm. This looked more like an extension of the concrete jungle that she saw around her. Kisha felt a sudden wave of homesickness. The campus was sprawling and students used cycles to move from one building to another. Kisha had opted for a private room. She was told even Anara had had a single room. She wondered if she was in the same wing as her sister, but with three hostels, it would have to be quite the coincidence. She wasn't sure yet.

Kisha's decision to enroll in the student exchange program wasn't just because of her curiosity to know what had happened to Anara. The itch to know the truth was there. But she was also somewhere driven by a certain guilt. The way Kisha saw it, it should've been her instead of Anara who moved to India with their father. That was what was decided between the sisters, but Anara changed it at the last minute, saying Kisha wouldn't be able to handle so much change in life all of a sudden. And now her elder sister was probably living the destiny that had been designed for her, Kisha thought. Anara wasn't only an elder sister to her. She was like her mother too. Truth be told, Kisha considered Anara more of a motherly figure than even Ranya. From her first toy, to her first book, to making her fight her fears, to educating her about her periods and how to use a sanitary napkin—it had all been Anara even though she was only a year and a half elder to Kisha. It was Anara who got

Kisha interested in protecting the environment as well. She was the wind beneath Kisha's wings. The safety bag in the car of her life. And now she wasn't there. Vanished. Kisha had six months to figure out the truth behind Anara's sudden disappearance and get some kind of emotional closure for her guilt, before it was time to head back to London.

After the admission procedure and paper work were done, Prithibi dropped Kisha at the hostel gate.

'Remember, I'm only a call away,' he said.

Kisha nodded, seeing her dad drive off. She had thought of asking him if the police had mentioned any Heartbreak Club during the investigation, but she didn't, fearing cross-questioning. She wanted to first know whether the anonymous message was a prank or had any substance to it.

Kisha found her room in the first floor of Wing B of the girls' hostel, at the end of a long corridor. The moment she entered, she noticed the room was decorated with balloons. A smile touched her face. She pulled her luggage and kept it beside the bed. There was a note pasted on the wooden wardrobe. It read: *Welcome Miss Achiever.* Kisha interpreted it to mean that the students were warm and welcoming. She looked up at the ceiling. Three balloons were attached to the fan, with one word written on each: *Surprise. Burst. Me.*

Intrigued, Kisha took off her hair clip, climbed the bed and, standing on her toes, reached the balloons. She pierced the three balloons, one at a time, in quick succession. Then she let out a scream as a heap of dead cockroaches fell on her.

TWO

KISHA KEPT SCREAMING AND SHAKING EVEN AFTER THE last cockroach was on the floor, but nobody came to help. She rushed to the attached washroom, scrubbed her face clean and finally calmed herself. *This has to be reported*, Kisha thought and dashed right out of her room and into the main corridor. She'd only taken a couple of steps when a voice stopped her.

'I wouldn't complain, if I were you.'

Kisha turned to notice a girl with short hair, leaning against a door. She was wearing pajamas which had small skulls printed all over. Kisha knew the look the girl was giving her. It screamed don't-mess-with-me. The girl walked up to her slowly. Kisha didn't know if she was being aggressive or friendly, till she saw her extend her hand. Kisha shook it.

'Kisha Sen,' she said with a tentative smile.

'Vega Pathak. I put the cockroaches in there.'

Kisha's smile vanished as Vega's words fell on her ears.

'Why would you do that?' She sounded pissed off.

'That's my way of welcoming any new entrant to this wing of the hostel. And *my* way is usually *our* way here.'

That said it all. Vega Pathak was the boss here. Kisha didn't know what to say. This was her first residential school experience. In London, she was a day scholar and would return home after attending school. Now she was on her own. She didn't have a mother or an elder sister to passive-aggressively bully the others into pampering her. At that moment Kisha realised life would not be the same as London. She would have to take certain decisions, and those decision would have consequences.

'If you complain, the hostel will turn against you. And then the cockroaches may appear in many other places, not just balloons,' Vega said.

She was walking away, when she turned to look at Kisha and said, 'Unless you have a thing for cockroaches.' A crooked smile slowly appeared on her face. She turned and walked away. Kisha stood there contemplating her options. Then she went inside her room and locked the main door from inside.

It took her an hour to clean the mess. After putting all the dead cockroaches in the bin—where had Vega even found them!—Kisha unpacked and bathed. What a first day it had been. She felt exhausted. Classes started from the next day and Kisha felt unprepared. She was already at a loss for time. One thing Kisha could never master was time management. She was always late for everything, and always needed that elusive extra hour in a day.

Finally feeling cosy in her pajamas, she Facetimed her mother in London. Ranya was having Irish coffee with her girl gang. She excused herself and went out to talk.

'Your dad messaged that he had made sure you were well settled in the hostel. I was waiting for your call. How is my little one doing? Everything good?' Ranya asked in one single breath. Kisha hated the tone she used whenever she referred to her as the 'little one'. It was as if Kisha was an imbecile who wouldn't understand the care in her if she used a normal tone.

She took three quick deep breaths as taught to her in rehab, to control her bubbling anger.

'I'm good, mom. Just getting used to everything.'

'Any issues so far?'

'Nay.' Kisha didn't want to mention anything and worry her mother. It was already quite late and the day had been long. She could feel sleep blurring her vision already.

'I just called to say I'm fine. I'll speak to you properly over the weekend. It's a packed schedule out here.'

'I get it, love. I have something to share with you.'

'What happened?' For a trice Kisha thought it was about Anara.

'I've had a talk with my boss here. I'll resign and take up a job in a five star hotel in Delhi. After what happened to Anara, I don't think I'll be able to sleep properly knowing you are in the same place and away from me. Being in Delhi, at least I'll be able to meet you often.'

Kisha realised her mother was also lonely, living all by herself in London. Just like she was feeling lonesome in life without Anara, her mother was too. *If you had done that earlier, Anara di and I would have been in the same city*, Kisha thought but said aloud, 'I would love that, mom, but my stay here is only for six months.'

'Just take care and know I'll be there real soon.' Ranya ended the call. Within a minute Kisha was fast asleep.

Deep into the night, the main door of Kisha's room clicked open. Vega crept into the room, without a sound. With her was Shruti, another girl from the hostel, who followed her in. Vega had duplicate keys to everyone's room. The two girls tiptoed inside and found the five small crates of mineral water that Kisha had kept on the floor, near the cupboard. This was something Vega had noticed when Kisha's father dropped her earlier in the day. Kisha had requested the guard below to bring the crates to her room. One by one the girls opened and emptied all the mineral water in the wash basin. They filled the bottles with tap water which was what everyone in the hostel drank. The tap water was centrally filtered for everyone. Then they tip toed out of the room. When Kisha woke up in the morning and reached for a water bottle, she noticed there was a note on one of the bottles which read:

We believe in equality. Let's all drink this disgusting tap water and be sick together, Miss Brit Brat.

The sarcasm made Kisha smile. She realised it was snobbish on her part to bring in the mineral water. In fact, she had felt awkward about it. But Ranya had insisted, telling her how dangerous drinking water in India was. In fact, nothing according to her mother was worth its salt in India even though she herself had grown up in the country, drinking the same water. Sometimes Kisha found it hard to shrug off the hypocrisy in her statements. Ranya, for Kisha, was a woman who loved to keep up with the trends and be hep. Kisha drank the water from the bottle, and leapt out of bed, prepping for the day.

The on-campus cycles were operated by an intra-school app. Kisha booked her cycle and when she went to the stand, close to the hostel building, she unlocked it using the unique code, flashing on the app. As she cycled to the academic building, where her classroom was, she noticed the central building of the school was such that the sun's morning rays fell on it, lighting it up in a wholesome manner. The logo and the name of the school shone bright in the sunlight. The weather in June wasn't harsh unlike what Ranya had told her to expect.

The sunshine was warm and there was a light breeze. She could see other students cycling to the main building but couldn't spot Vega. Kisha had learnt a lesson back in London during her rehab. When you can't fight your enemy, befriend them. Had it been the Kisha before rehab, goodness knows what her anger would have made her do to Vega, knowing she was the one who had subjected her to the cockroaches. But the new Kisha had tools to deal with her rage. She could feel it within her that she had changed for the better.

As Kisha reached her classroom, she saw a few students sitting around. Ranya had warned her that she could find the number of students in class overwhelming. 'India has a whopping population so it's going to be a crowded classroom,' she had said. Kisha counted twenty-one students. Again, it was a fact contrary to what Ranya had told her.

Kisha had the urge to Facetime her mother right then and there and tell her that she needed to check her facts about her own homeland, but using phones during class hours was against the school rules. The phones had to be on airplane mode and safely inside the student lockers. Kisha's locker and keys had been allotted to her the day before, when her father had dropped her. It was part of the orientation box which was given to every student. The box contained a lot of paraphernalia about the school, its rules and regulations, the locker number and key along with some club membership documents and direction to download the school app.

On the school app, Kisha discovered that she had been assigned a captain. Apparently, every new student had a captain assigned to them in Fairmont High. A captain was a senior who was supposed to supervise their junior's actions and initiate them in the ways of the school. They were supposed to be their first go-to person in case of any issue within the school campus. A few girls asked her who her captain was. When she showed them the name, she heard a collective sigh from the girls. It made her frown in puzzlement. But she understood the reason when she met him during recess. She didn't have to look for him. He came to her class looking for her.

And when he stood in front of Kisha, she realised she hadn't seen a guy with such a perfect jawline and such bewitching eyes before. This boy was her captain. This boy was ... Tavish Mathur. But the first thing he asked her, jolted her out of her dreamy reverie.

'Aren't you Anara's little sister?'

THREE

For the first time, the ever so vocal Kisha was finding it difficult to speak. Was it because of Tavish's magnetic presence? Was is that her brain only wanted to register him and not focus on the words which were expected of her? Kisha didn't know. And frankly, she couldn't be bothered either. She managed to nod her head.

'Thought so. I remember her showing me a picture of you,' he said.

Thank goodness he answered before I had to ask, Kisha thought, tongue-tied as she was. She found her bearings and finally asked, 'But how do you know her?'

'Anara was my class mate.'

The 'was' part hurt. *Should I ask about Anara? If he knows anything about what could've happened to her? About the Heartbreak Club? Or should I wait?* Kisha wondered.

'I'm here as part of the student exchange programme,' Kisha said. She would talk more about Anara later, she'd decided.

'Alright. And now you're under me.'

The 'under me' part was loaded. Kisha was about to get some intimate visuals when she controlled her mind and brought it back to where her body was. In school. In front of her captain.

'I hope you know 20 per cent of your overall marks depend on how your captain grades you.'

'I do.'

'Do behave then. And follow the rules.'

'I don't know the rules.'

Tavish rolled his eyes.

'I don't know why the authorities do only half the work. Anyway, rule number one is that you don't go out of the school campus without telling me. Rule number two is you come to me first if you have any kind of problem. Like any kind! Rule number three is never try to pull a fast one on me. Make sense?'

'Pretty much.'

'Good. I did go through your Wiki page. A young achiever, huh?'

'Thanks for Googling me,' Kisha said cheekily.

'Every day we meet for half an hour in the morning before classes and half an hour after classes.'

'Where?'

'In the shower?'

'Excuse me?' Kisha thought she'd heard it wrong.

'The campus shower in the pool area, obviously.'

He has a sense of humor too. He better not have more qualities or else ... Kisha stopped her train of thought and heard him say, 'I'll ping you via the school app.'

'Okay.'

Tavish turned and walked a few steps. Kisha's eyes were on him, admiring his easy, ambling gait. He turned again, to look at her and said rather loudly, 'Do not look at me when I'm not looking at you.'

'Is that a rule?' Kisha asked, unable to hold back. Pre-rehab, impulsive Kisha seemed to be making a comeback.

Tavish came back to her. This time he stood closer than before and then he hissed under his breath, 'More of a warning, sweeto.'

On another day, Kisha would have retaliated with an acerbic come-back, but she didn't know what sealed her lips at that moment. Was it the boy? Was it the fact that he was her captain? Was it that he had said he knew Anara? What was it? But what her mind noted was if she went by the rules with this one, it would all be boring. That turn around, that proximity and the way he had said 'Sweeto' sharply ... she wanted to re-experience it all.

The rest of the day was slow. When classes got over, Kisha decided to cycle to the library. She picked a few books, heard certain audio books on environmental conservation and then decided to make her way back to the hostel. While cycling back to her room, she passed the rugby ground. Tavish was running with the ball while some other boys were chasing him. He was wearing soccer-shorts. Kisha's eyes didn't want to but, steered by her hormones, they went to his thighs. The way his muscular legs were flexing as he outran the others, created a funny feeling within her. Before things became more complex, she chose to cycle to the hostel fast.

Every hostel wing had a huge common dining area on its terrace. Students were required to have their breakfast, lunch and dinner together in this space. Kisha took her food-tray and sat in a corner. Girls of all shapes and sizes flooded the dining area. Most of them were in groups. Kisha wondered if the person who had messaged her anonymously about Anara and the group was here too. The Heartbreak Club. What could it be about? Suddenly her eyes fell on Vega, who was sitting a few tables away. Kisha stood up with her tray and approached her.

'Hey!' she said.

Vega was surrounded by three girls. One of them was Shruti.

'If it isn't Brat Brit,' Vega said. 'How is it going?'

'Good. Wanted to thank you for the note last night. And the shot of reality,' Kisha said.

Vega gave her a smirk, noticing she wasn't carrying a mineral water bottle.

'May I join you guys?' Kisha asked.

'Why?' Shruti asked.

'Why not? Everyone wants company right?'

'Okay, you can sit with us,' Vega said. Kisha sat down beside one of the girls. The group started chit-chatting amongst themselves, making Kisha feel like an outsider. With nobody even caring to glance at her, Kisha suddenly blurted out, 'So, who runs this Heartbreak Club?'

There was an abrupt silence. Vega looked at Kisha and said, 'Never ever take that name again.' She stood up and walked away. The other girls followed her. They went and sat in another part of the area, away from Kisha. Without even talking about it, Kisha learnt something about the club—the club was real and that it was forbidden. The anonymous message mentioning it wasn't a joke after all. *So, what about that part of the message which stated THC's role in Anara going missing? Was that true too?* Kisha had a sinking feel in her gut.

FOUR

AS SHE WAS COMING DOWN THE TERRACE, A THOUGHT struck Kisha. Anara must have stayed in the same hostel while she was in school. The wing could be different but the place was the same. Could her room yield any clues about her disappearance? She didn't know whether the police had searched her room or not. Maybe they had. Maybe not. Kisha had to find out. She went to the reception on the ground floor.

'I'm Kisha Sen, one of the exchange students from London. My sister studied here: Anara Sen. She disappeared eight months ago. Would it be possible to know which room she stayed in?'

The lady behind the desk didn't look the fussy type. She quickly typed something and looked at the computer screen in front of her. Then she looked up at Kisha.

'You're her sister, you said?'

'That's right, ma'am. Here is my id,' Kisha said with a sweet smile.

'Fine. Anara Sen was in room number 117.'

Kisha swallowed a lump. It was the same room as hers. 117.

'Are you sure?'

This time the woman gave her a sharp glance. Clearly, she didn't like people challenging her. Kisha quickly got the drift and nodded. She went up to her room—Anara's room too—

number 117. As she entered it, she could feel a different vibe within its four walls. Knowing that her missing sister had lived in this same room, had changed something. She'd checked the room last night. Ranya had alerted her about hidden cameras, so she had done a thorough sweep. She had found nothing. Kisha checked the room once again, hoping against hope to find something that was Anara's this time. A clue or a hint. But again, she found nothing. A dejected Kisha sat on her bed, thinking.

If the Heartbreak Club was indeed so secretive and scary that people didn't even like mentioning their name, then how would I know who belongs to the club? Or should I just start talking to more people about it? Was Anara a part of the club too, or was she only a victim like the anonymous message stated? Kisha wondered. In the months that had lapsed since she came back from rehab and realised Anara was missing, she had been restless. Something wasn't letting her be at peace even though she continued to pursue her school and regular life in London. Anara's disappearance was always there on her conscious track. There were times when she lulled herself to sleep after staring at Anara's social media and WhatsApp for hours, hoping she would be online. She was determined to find out what had happened to Anara from day one, but she didn't know how to go about it. Her parents had given up on it or so she thought. What do you do when even the police had no answers? She didn't completely blame her parents. An hour after Kisha had received the anonymous message, telling her about Anara's disappearance and the Heartbreak Club, Kisha had been sitting with her mother with tears of disbelief running down her eyes.

'One of Anara's friends left me a message,' Kisha said without sharing anything more with her mother. But she had a pertinent and emotional query for Ranya.

'When were you guys planning to tell me?' she screamed. She was feeling gutted. When your own family hides serious things from you, the only thing you can or should do, after recovering from the shock, is confront them.

'Kish, you were in rehab. You just came home today. I didn't want to pile on more on you immediately—'

'Oh come on, mom, spare me that. Tell me what happened to Anara di? Where is she?'

The kind of pause Ranya took, told Kisha something bad was coming.

'We ... we don't know. Not even your father. Two months back he got a phone call from the school telling him that she was nowhere to be found.'

'What do you mean nowhere to be found? Didn't she live on campus?'

'Exactly my reaction. Your dad reported the matter to the police, of course. They investigated for a couple of months quite seriously but there was nothing to go on. No clue came out of it. After the initial months, they just wanted to close the case and move on. They told your father that perhaps Anara disappeared on her own. And people who go away willfully are difficult to track.'

'And you both accepted it?' Kisha said rubbing her eyes.

'If we had accepted it, the case would have been closed by now. Prithibi is in touch with the officer who was in charge of the case. She told him that since the children of wealthy and important people study in that school, they were under pressure to hush up the investigation and not bring bad publicity to the school. The police have their personnel doing their bit. The main problem is we aren't sure if she could've actually just gone off on her own. Till we have something concrete we can only follow up. You have to understand that beyond this, there's nothing much we can do. This isn't a Bollywood film, dear. This is real life.'

Like hell it is real life, thought Kisha. She was shocked at her mother's words. Was it possible that Ranya didn't care? Kisha didn't see the worry in her mother's eyes, the way she herself felt it. Could it be, perhaps, because she was the one who had received the anonymous message and not her mom. Not even her dad. Or the police. Were adults this good at accepting such things? Kisha decided not to tell her mother about the message she had received. If they didn't care, why should they know?

Moreover, going by Ranya, it was evident there were powerful people who were trying to save the school's reputation. Mentioning the anonymous message and the Heartbreak Club, without knowing much about it, may mess things up. The members could be forewarned and they could tamper with the truth. It was then that Kisha understood there was only one way to find out what had happened to Anara: she herself had to go there keeping her intentions hidden.

'So, if I go missing, you and dad will simply accept it and move on?' A hurt Kisha asked. Ranya made her sit down, clasped her hand and, looking at her kindly, said, 'We haven't moved on, Kish. We also want to find Anara. Let me repeat myself. The police are still investigating. And they have assured us, the moment they find out anything about her disappearance, they are going to inform us about it. Your dad is also asking them from time to time. Till then all we can do is wait. But just because we are waiting doesn't mean we don't care. To wait is also a step in the right direction.' Kisha took a deep breath and decided not to argue further with her mother.

Now that she was actually in Fairmont High International, Noida, Kisha understood that in all probability the Heartbreak Club wasn't really a typical school club. There had to be more to the club. Vega had acted positively shady when Kisha had tried to ask about it. Then, a final thought hovered in her mind: Why was the anonymous message sent only to her? Why not to her parents or the police? *Maybe because the sender knew I would do something about Anara di's disappearance. Or is someone waiting for me here, who knew I would come here to find out more?* The answer scared her.

Soon it was time to go up to the terrace for dinner. This time she didn't see Vega or any of her groupies. Kisha finished her food in solitude, observing the students around her, and came down to her room. As she lay down, she opened the school app on her phone. There was a student portal within the app where any insider could search for a particular student by name to check their school profile. Kisha punched in Anara's name. Immediately a message popped up on the screen: *Information about this student is no longer available.*

She found the removal of her sister's profile rather insensitive. It had not been a whole year since her disappearance. If she had really vanished of her own free will, she would definitely return one day. The assumption that she wouldn't, was disturbing for Kisha. Her mind went blank for a trice. Then another name popped up in her head. She typed in the search bar: Tavish Mathur. His profile opened up in front of her. The guy was a school jock, no doubt, but he also seemed to be an all-rounder. He had won awards in sports, music, academics ... the list was long. Kisha went through the classes he attended apart from his basic academics. She smiled to herself on seeing that they had a class in common: music. She made a mental note of it before retiring to bed.

The next day, Kisha walked into music class full of expectation. She had enrolled for piano lessons while she knew, from snooping on the app the previous night, that Tavish played the guitar. *As if the jawline and eyes weren't enough*, Kisha thought seeing him practise on an electric guitar in the music room. The class was open to students across batches. One just had to opt for the time slot via the app and show up on time for their lesson. When Tavish noticed Kisha, he stopped playing his guitar and gestured her to come up to him. Kisha took nervous steps and stood by him. She had to look up at him because he was sitting on a slight pedestal with his guitar.

'Good that you are into music,' Tavish said locking eyes with her.

Don't do that, Kisha's mind screamed, seeing his eyes piercing into hers, but what came out was, 'Yeah, it calms me down.'

'Which instrument brings you here?' Tavish asked.

'I like to play the king,' Kisha said, knowing well that it sounded rather flirtatious. Tavish gave her an enquiring look.

Kisha clarified. 'The piano? It is the king of musical instruments, in my opinion.'

Tavish nodded and got back to his guitar.

'I checked your profile, by the way,' Kisha said, not ready to give up his hard-won attentions. 'It's really impressive. Back in London people said I had such a profile but look at yours. Is there anything you are not into?' she said, already sounding like a fan girl.

Tavish gently strummed the guitar a couple of times, looked arrow-straight at her again and said, 'I'm not in to you.' There was a slight smile which Kisha couldn't interpret—was it plain arrogance or was it flirtatious?

Yet, Kisha chose to complete in her mind. Tavish played on. She went and took her seat by the piano in the adjacent, sound proof room. Her fingers were shaking as she found her note... *not into you* ... The way he had said it, she felt as if it was almost a challenge thrown at her. Claim me if you can, it seemed to say. Those words had shifted something within her. Kisha blushed to herself wondering if he had said the same thing to any other girl.

As the day progressed, Kisha made sure to approach the teachers who had taught Anara from the time she was studying here. She also spoke to some of her batchmates though she steered clear of Tavish. To her confusion, everyone had a different version of Anara. At times it felt like she was getting glimpses of the sister she knew and loved, and at other times Kisha felt she was hearing stuff that was about a completely different person. Was Anara's mental health affected for some reason? Did it trigger her disappearance? Was the Heartbreak Club a means to do that? She realised she would have to take some steps to reach the club members, or else she could spend a lifetime here and not find out anything about it. Nobody brought it up on their own. It was clearly an underground club. Even the teachers gave her very similar reactions to the students.

'Who told you about that club? Don't waste time on such things,' said one of Anara's teacher.

'All that is baseless. There's no such club here,' said another.

'If there was such a club, you think they wouldn't have been busted by now?' said yet another. The response didn't help Kisha one bit in her pursuit.

The next morning when Kisha woke up, she realised her phone was missing. When she went to open the main door, there was a note: *Phone is in the boys' locker room. No complaints, remember, Brat Brit.* Kisha knew it had to be Vega. Kisha quickly got into a pair of shorts and pulled a t shirt over her head.

The boys' locker room was adjacent to the swimming pool area. The girls' locker room was to the right of the boys' locker room. Kisha cycled her way to the outside of the swimming pool building. It was an indoor pool. When she reached, she realised there were very few students around. She wasn't surprised, it wasn't even time for breakfast yet. Kisha parked her cycle and went inside. With any luck, the boys' locker room would be empty right now.

She hesitated in front of the locker room door. She couldn't hear any sounds from inside. *It must be empty*, she thought and realised she had to seize her chance. She dashed right inside. Then came out with equal urgency. How the hell was she supposed to find her phone inside that huge locker room.

She ran out to the guard sitting outside the swimming pool building.

'May I have your phone please?' Kisha said. The guard would have never given his phone to a boy but girls, he believed, were better souls. And this one looked desperate. He handed over his smart phone to her. Kisha dialled her number. When she heard her phone ring, she gave the guard his phone back.

'Please don't end the call till I come out,' she requested and dashed inside again. She could hear the phone ring. The more she rushed towards the sound, the louder the sound got, till she entered the locker room and figured the sound was coming from inside one of the changing rooms, behind a thick curtain. As she pushed the curtain to a side, Kisha's heart was in her mouth. Tavish was standing there holding her phone which was ringing loudly. But that was not the point. The point was that he was butt naked.

FIVE

'WHAT THE HELL ARE YOU DOING HERE, KISHA SEN?' TAVISH raised his voice.

'I didn't see anything, I swear!' Kisha said with her eyes wide open. Then she realised the contradiction in what she was saying and what she was doing and closed her eyes.

'Shut up! This is the boys' locker room. If you had to meet me, there are other more appropriate places.'

Kisha barely opened one of her eyes and noticed he had clumsily wrapped the curtain around his waist, sort of like a makeshift sarong. She relaxed and opened her eyes.

'I know and I never would've barged in like that on any other day, but I didn't have a choice. I had to come here for my phone.'

'Your what?' Tavish asked confused. Then, as if suddenly realising it, he looked from her to the phone he was holding. He flung it at her the next instant. Kisha caught it and ended the call. The guard outside had dutifully kept the phone ringing.

'You want to explain what your phone is doing here? Are you recording in the boys' locker room?'

'No! I'm not a perv.'

'At this point, I am not sure I believe you.'

'Some girls from my hostel played a prank on me. They hid my phone here and—'

'Hold on. Nothing is making sense. And it won't make sense till I'm naked here in front of you.'

'Well, yeah. That doesn't help either.'

'What doesn't?'

'You pronouncing your nudity. I know you are naked, but I don't want to hear it because I am already seeing it. Saying it is only making me imagine you—'

'But you said you didn't see anything!'

'Not yours. But I do know what a di—'

'Stop right there!'

'Looks like in general,' Kisha said, her words dying out at the end.

'Can you just get the hell out of here before someone comes in?'

'Right, of course,' Kisha said. She waved awkwardly in Tavish's direction and rushed out holding her phone tight.

It was hard for Kisha to focus in class that day. She kept replaying the scene in her head—walking in on a very naked Tavish—and cringed with embarrassment. She also knew that had Tavish been caught inside the girls' locker room, then things could've turned very ugly. By the time her classes ended, she decided she would not only personally apologise to Tavish but also confront Vega. What, after all, was the point of all this harassment? Kisha pinged Tavish via the school messenger. He responded and agreed to meet her by the rugby field.

When Kisha reached the spot, Tavish was already in his

rugby uniform. On spotting her, he excused himself and jogged up to her.

'Tell me.'

'I just want to apologise.'

'For?'

'For whatever happened this morning.'

'But didn't you say you were pranked?'

'I was, but still.'

'Alright, apology accepted. Anything else?'

I wish I had a list, Kisha thought. 'No.'

'Cool. I'm kind of in the middle of a game so if you don't mi—'

'You know anything about the Heartbreak Club?' Kisha blurted out what was on her mind. Clearly, if she had given it some thought, she would've stayed mum.

Tavish was about to turn to join his teammates when he stopped and looked at her long and hard. He came closer and, as if he weighing his words carefully, said, 'Who told you about the club?'

'I ... I...' Kisha fumbled for an excuse. She didn't want to tell him about the anonymous message.

'Whatever. Don't bother to lie to me. Just remember, whoever told you about the club, stay away from them.'

Kisha wanted to ask what he meant but Tavish turned on his heel and ran towards the field. She was looking at his receding figure when suddenly he turned his head and stared at her before joining his team mates. What did that mean? Kisha was confused. She cycled away from the place, Tavish's last look etched in her mind. There was an uneasiness within, which she couldn't negate since she had met Tavish.

That night, Kisha skipped dinner. She kept tossing and turning and thinking about the events of the day. By the wee hours of the morning, she was famished. She had nothing in her room and the terrace canteen, was closed. The eatery opened at 7 a.m. She somehow controlled her hunger and the moment it was 7, Kisha was the first one to be there. She took her tray and was looking for a place to sit when she spotted something written on a table. She went to it. And when she read what was written, her head reeled.

LOOKING FOR US, K?

The message was scratched on the table, and the three O's in it were made of real human hair. Kisha didn't know if it was hers or not, but the sight of it filled her with nausea. Then she heard the canteen manager, a beefy Haryanvi who went by the name of Ballu Pa, shout out her name. Ballu was short for Balwinder Punia while Pa was short for Paaji, which in Punjabi meant big brother.

'Kisha Sen?'

Kisha turned and went up to him.

'This was here,' he said, pointing to a piece of paper with her name on it.

It was a note and her name was written on one side of the folded paper. On the other side was the name of a classic book.

Kisha swallowed a lump in her throat after reading it. Suddenly the hunter had turned into the hunted.

THE HEARTBREAK CLUB: CHAT FILES – 1

NOBODY KNEW, BUT FAIRMONT HIGH INTERNATIONAL'S school app had been hacked by the Heartbreak Club a year after it was officially launched. And it is within the app that they started their own digital meetings without anyone getting a whiff of it. Like always, today too a new chat box popped up on the school app. Five people with different names—King, Bishop, Rook, Knight, Pawn—joined in. A Virtual Private Network (VPN) was used to initiate such chats, so even if someone tried, it was next to impossible to track the IP.

KING: All here?

KNIGHT: I am.

BISHOP: I am.

ROOK: Me too.

KING: Where's Queen?

KNIGHT: Don't know. She didn't join the last three times either.

KING: I know that. I'll check with Queen. Anyway, what's the latest about Kisha Sen?

ROOK: I did what was required. Gave her the heads up. Will communicate with her soon. But do you think it is safe to get Kisha in?

KING: I don't think she can be harmful for us even if we offer her to join us. She fits the requirement. High IQ and all that.

KNIGHT: I concur.

BISHOP: I figured out that she is into Tavish Mathur. He is her captain as well.

KING: So? A lot of girls are into Tavish Mathur? What's the point?

PAWN: I think Bishop is hinting at Anara's inclination towards Tavish. And now Kisha.

KING: Are we here to discuss people's love stories?

BISHOP: Sorry, King.

PAWN: Sorry, King.

KNIGHT: It's obvious someone has told her something connects Anara to the club. Else she wouldn't have asked about the club from the moment she came in.

KING: Exactly. But Kisha's snooping around shouldn't activate the police. That's our only concern.

ROOK: I so agree. This Anara thing made us lie low for so many months. Finally it died down. Can't re-open it all.

PAWN: But we did well to keep Anara's disappearance under wraps even when the police interrogated us not knowing we are part of the club.

KNIGHT: Exactly. Our balls were tight on that.

BISHOP: So, you *are* a guy, Knight?

KNIGHT: Haha. No, I'm a straight girl. Happy?

KING: Enough. Any other observation or should we dissolve?

ROOK: Don't you think we are giving her the black handshake a little too easily?

KING: But look at the fatal side. By offering her the black handshake, we would push her to sell her soul. There's no coming back after that.

If it was a real life meet, each member would have had a

devilish smirk on their face, as they knew exactly what the King was hinting at.

KING: Until next time, let's dissolve.

One by one everyone logged out of the room. And the room ceased to exist.

SIX

KISHA IMMEDIATELY ASKED BALLU PA ABOUT THE NOTE and the message scratched out on the table, but he said he didn't know much more about them. Both things were there before he'd opened the canteen in the morning. Later that day, Kisha got in touch with the tech support of the school and checked the CCTV footage of the canteen area.

'I've misplaced an important document and I remember I still had it when I was in the canteen. Just wanted to check if anyone picked it up by mistake,' Kisha had told the tech guy.

She checked the video footage and figured there was a forty-five second jump around a certain time in the morning after which, she noticed, the writing on the table had magically appeared. Though it was difficult to spot the note from the camera's view, it was a no brainer that the forty-five second jump had happened exactly when the writing and 'appeared' on the table. The CCTV must have been tampered with. And Kisha was sure it was the members of the Heartbreak Club who had done this.

At breakfast the next day, Vega approached Kisha while she was sitting by herself and eating her muesli.

'Wow, we have such similar tastes. I love muesli too,' Vega said in a saccharine voice. Kisha noticed her groupies weren't with her but were lurking at a distance. And this overtly friendly vibe wasn't what she expected of Vega after their past encounters. Without even caring to ask if she could sit next to her, Vega sat there with a stupid smile on her face. It was evident she needed something from Kisha.

'Cough it up,' Kisha said, rolling her eyes and spooning some muesli into her mouth. The smile disappeared from Vega's face as she realised Kisha wasn't buying her act anyway.

'Thanks. It wasn't coming to me naturally.'

'I know.' There was mild amusement on Kisha's face.

'I'll come to the point. I tried my best but couldn't get Tavish as my captain. But you did.'

'Without even trying,' Kisha said. She knew she could have avoided saying it but the bitch in her had suited-up, sensing she had some leverage over Vega.

'That's plain luck. Anyway, I have this crazy ass crush on him. And I want you to fill him in about me.'

'What about you?'

'Good stuff, obviously, so he gets attracted to me.'

Kisha gave her a glance and said, 'Oh, you mean I have to create good stuff about you and lie to him?'

Vega realised what Kisha was trying to do. She was getting back at her for the phone thing without even stating it.

'This is the only way you can earn my friendship,' Vega said.

'I get it. Fine, I'll talk to Tavish.'

'Good girl.' Vega stood up.

'But no more pranks on me,' Kisha said it almost as an ultimatum. Vega glanced at her, weighing whether she should snap back, and then said, 'Alright.'

Vega headed towards her groupies when she heard Kisha say aloud for the entire bunch of students present there to listen, 'Thanks for assuming that I care about earning your friendship, Vega.' She smirked as Vega gave her a brief, hateful look before strutting away. Her groupies followed.

It was a Sunday, and Sundays at Fairmont High were for parents and guardians to come to school and meet their wards. Sometimes the students were allowed to leave the campus with a written permission from their parents or local guardian, to go and meet them. Kisha had not expected her father to show up. He had called up once during the week and that itself had felt like a lot on his part. Thus, she was surprised when she found out that he was there to see her.

Kisha met him in the administrative block.

'How is my girl doing? Fitting in well?' Prithibi asked.

'Tell me, dad, how many times did you come to meet Anara di here?' Kisha couldn't hold back her feelings.

For the next two seconds, Prithibi's remorseful face held the answer to Kisha's question. But then, pretense took over.

'Of course, I used to visit. What do you mean by how many times? I can't keep a count of such things.'

'Don't lie, dad. I checked the register. You only came once. That too three months after Anara di had been admitted here. You put her here and forgot all about her.'

This time Prithibi simply hung his head in shame.

'If you had been in touch with her at least you would have known what was going on in her life. Forget that, even after her disappearance you simply didn't care enough to look for her. All because the police told you she had supposedly gone off on her own. "Supposedly." And you bought it!'

Prithibi was about to talk when his phone rang. He answered it.

'I'll call you right back, baby.'

Kisha immediately knew who it was. His new girlfriend. That sound of her father labelling another lady as 'baby' in front of her changed her visage instantly. Kisha felt even more disgusted. Not only did he not care about Anara or her, he had wasted no time in starting a fresh life for himself. It was almost as if he couldn't wait to forget them and start anew.

'We have spoken about this, Kisha,' Prithibi said. 'There's nothing more I could have done. This isn't a movie and I'm not Liam Neeson who will go out and hunt for his missing daughter.'

'You aren't Liam Neeson, I agree, but you are a father, aren't you? Tell me why you gave up so easily, dad.'

Prithibi tried hard, but he couldn't look Kisha in the eye. How could he tell his daughter that he felt completely detached from his own family or that he was so busy wooing the woman he had recently fallen in love with that he had ignored his elder daughter? Even if he did confess, it would lead to Kisha hating him in an irreversible way. But the quieter he remained, the more furious Kisha became. His silence was damaging their relationship more than his words might have. His phone rang again. It was his girlfriend, probably upset at him for not speaking to her properly the first time she had called. Kisha looked at him and rolled her eyes.

Prithibi took the call again and mildly repeated what he had said half a minute back. When he ended the call, Kisha was glaring at him.

'If that had been mom you would have lost your cool with her, fought with her and most probably blocked her for a few hours as well. The truth is dad, you never had time for us,' Kisha said, raising her voice. Prithibi stood there for some time trying to salvage the meeting and chit chat about frivolous things. But Kisha had had enough. 'Just stop,' she screamed and stalked off. Realising he had hit a dead-end, Prithibi left. Kisha's reaction wasn't unexpected for him. Anara had had similar things to say to him.

Kisha was feeling triggered. She felt let down by her father. She realised that he had already replaced them in his life and that thought upset and angered her. The one thing she had been taught in rehab was to look for a non-violent vent when she felt triggered. Kisha took a deep breath and practised the 4-7-8 breathing pattern. By the time she felt relaxed she knew exactly what she had to do in the next hour.

She went to the school's swimming club and headed straight to the changing room. She slipped into her swimsuit and went to the pool. There were a few students in the water already. Kisha dove in. It was only after she had finished a few continuous laps that she felt slightly better. She was thinking of getting out and taking a break when she heard a commotion. She swam up to the corner, where the noise seemed to come from, and raised her body out of the pool. A few boys surrounded a thin, nerdy guy and seemed to be bullying him. He was trying to protect himself in a defeated way and looked totally punctured of confidence. Kisha didn't get why they were bullying him, but on an impulse, she yelled out, 'Hey! What's the problem?'

The boys stopped. The bullied boy shivered in a corner.

'Not your business,' said one of the bullies. Kisha walked up to them.

'That may be right but I can make it my own in one second. And when I do, I won't stop till each one of you gets suspended.'

'Listen here—' The boy charged at her a little aggressively. Kisha simply gripped his shoulder with both hands and kneed him between his legs. He screamed out in pain.

'Never approach a girl aggressively. If you don't know how to approach a girl, I will talk to the principal and request that you be given private tuitions.'

The other boys took a few steps back. Kisha looked at the nerdy guy who stood in a corner, staring at her.

'What's happening here?' she asked.

'They … they are forcing me to swim naked,' the boy replied meekly. Kisha looked back at the bullies and said, 'If you don't disperse in the next five seconds, your fantasy will be served to the principal.' Kisha stood with her hands on her hips. The boys, one by one, moved out of her sight.

'Thanks,' the scrawny boy said.

'No problem,' Kisha said with a shrug and turned to proceed to the changing room. As she walked in, she noticed a pair of eyes following her every move. It was a girl, around her age, peeping out of one of the changing booths. She looked at Kisha in awe and smiled.

'Hi! I'm Jasmine. But you can call me Jas.'

'Kisha Sen.'

'Can we be friends?'

Kisha stopped in her tracks and looked at the girl. For the first time since she had come to India had she heard those words come out of anyone. The girl seemed sincere and genuine.

'I'm in your class. And I saw what you did. Good that you stepped in and saved Ahaan.'

Kisha frowned. Was the nerdy boy called Ahaan? The name sounded familiar. *Is he in my class?* Kisha wondered and then heard Jasmine clarify.

'Ahaan is in our class too. The poor guy is a soft target. People are always after his life because he doesn't fit in.'

'The world is a difficult place for those who don't fit in. It's just how it is. But anyway, nice to meet you, Jas.'

'Could you teach me the butterfly stroke?' Jas asked suddenly. 'Sorry, I was watching you swim. You look like a pro.'

'Thanks. I'll be glad to help.' Kisha smiled.

For the next two hours, she helped Jas learn the butterfly stroke. Tired after the long swimming session, when the two returned to the changing room again, Kisha asked Jas with a serious face, 'Do you know anything about the Heartbreak Club?'

Jas was mum, though Kisha thought she did notice her throwing a furtive glance around her. After a long pause, Jas said, 'It's kind of a secret club within the school. Nobody knows much about it. But it has been here for more than a decade, or so I've heard. Old students choose new ones to carry on the legacy.'

'What's their legacy anyway?'

Jas looked like she was on the verge of replying but then she looked at Kisha and said, 'I don't know.'

Suddenly a female voice boomed on the public address

intercom, making Jas and Kisha jump: 'This announcement is for Tavish Mathur, 12A. Wherever you are, please report to the administrative building. Your parents are here to meet you. Thank you.'

Kisha wondered where her captain could be. As they walked out of the swimming club, she noticed it was raining.

'I knew it would rain,' said Jas and held the umbrella high, while both cycled in a way that their heads weren't getting completely drenched. As they were passing the rugby field, Kisha noticed a figure sitting alone in the bleachers, getting drenched in the rain.

'Isn't that …?'

'Yeah, it's Tavish Mathur. Your captain, I suppose,' Jas said.

'You go ahead. I'll be right there,' Kisha said as Jas cycled on while Kisha parked her bike and ran to Tavish.

'Captain, your parents are here. They announced your name on the public announcement system,' she said catching her breath.

Tavish turned to look at her and said, 'Leave me alone. And don't tell them I'm here. They will bug me. I want to be left alone. They don't know.' It was a mutter now, 'Nobody knows that I killed my brother.' Then he looked up at the cloudy sky and murmured, 'Except myself.'

Kisha stood there, confused.

SEVEN

KISHA WAS BORED OF THE BURGERS AND HOT DOGS SHE had been eating since she had arrived at Fairmont High International, Noida. Today, she decided, she would have salad for lunch. She picked out a super green salad with avocado and edamame. As she went to get the cutlery, a stack of white plastic spoons and forks awaited her. Kisha rolled her eyes.

'Ballu Pa,' she called out, waving her arms to get his attention. 'Didn't I complain about the use of plastic cutlery here and you said you would talk to the authority. What happened?'

Ballu came to her and said in a heavy Haryanvi accent, 'Nobody listens to me. Anyway, cutlery is cutlery. Who cares what material it is made of. I can assure it's clean.'

'This is ridiculous,' Kisha said, exasperated.

'You don't have to be woke about everything, Brit brat,' came a voice from behind her. It was Vega and she was picking up a plastic fork.

'I would say sometimes being woke really helps. Plastic isn't good.'

'Oh, get off your high horse.' Vega was about to pick another plastic fork when Kisha held her hand. Vega looked at her in shock, she hadn't expected this.

'Let's take a collective stand. I'm sure the principal will hear us out.'

'In your dreams,' Vega said, shaking Kisha's grip off. She pierced her salad with the plastic fork and put it in her mouth with a do-whatever-you-can expression.

The students around started laughing. Kisha looked at them and realised all of them held plastic spoons and forks that they were using to eat their breakfast. The look on their face made her feel all the more humiliated. She kept her salad on the counter and walked out.

The morning assembly was about to conclude when the principal walked up on stage to address the students. Dr Sundaram Vishnu Iyer was a big man with a sizeable girth. The mic barely reached his mouth so he bent down slightly and cleared his throat. He looked the scholarly type and his perfect English had a twinge of a Tamil accent.

'Students, something important happened today. Something which made me question myself as well. For that I want to thank our exchange student, Kisha Sen.'

Kisha suddenly felt a lot of eyes on her, but she was unperturbed. She was used to eye balls. But she did look squarely at Vega who was looking at her from her spot in the queue.

Dr Iyer continued, 'This morning Kisha brought a very pertinent issue to my attention. The staff of Fairmont High International know how concerned I am about the environment and yet, we have not given a thought to the use of plastic on our campus, especially in our cafeteria. We don't stand for anything which can cause problems to our climate now or in the future. In fact, we are the only international school which doesn't use or encourage the use of air conditioners. We use traditional coolers. But somehow the things that are right in front of us get missed.

'Anyway, I wanted to thank Ms Kisha Sen for coming to me with her concerns. I would have loved it if someone who studied here had noticed and brought the issue to me, rather than an exchange student. Nevertheless, she is a part of the Fairmont High universe. Starting today, we will discontinue all plastic in the cafeteria and I will encourage you all to minimise your use of plastic. Here as well as in your homes. Let's appreciate Kisha's intent with a round of applause. May this inspire others to act upon pro-climatic things.'

The entire assembly, from the first to the twelfth standard, broke into thunderous applause for a good half thirty seconds.

'You may all disperse now. Thanks.'

As the assembly dispersed with students going to their own classrooms, Tavish came up to Kisha.

'Congrats. Looks like you are going to be popular here as well.'

'Thanks. I didn't do it to win popularity votes though.'

'Whatever. You should have come to me before going to the principal. I wouldn't have shared your credit for sure.'

Kisha knew Tavish had a point. The rules said she should bring up all her concerns with her captain first. It was only her heat-of-the-moment impulse that had made her walk straight to the principal from the canteen.

'Sorry.'

'First thanks and then sorry? That's some range,' Tavish said.
'Both were genuine though.'
'I know. By the way, I hope you haven't told anyone what I said about my brother yesterday?'
'I may have anger management issues but I don't have stupidity management issues.'

Tavish smirked and shook his head. He had been teetering on the verge of depression the day before. His energy was at an all-time low and he had no desire to face people. He camouflaged it as teenage angst and told people his parents depressed him. But only he knew the truth.

Tavish Mathur was from Ahmedabad. His father ran a business while his mother managed the house. They were among the most influential families in Gujarat because of his father's political connections. Keeping up appearances and maintaining their social standing was very important to his family. And one of the ways they used to do so was by flaunting Viren; Tavish's twin brother, older than him by two minutes.

They definitely had the golden child syndrome, when it came to Viren. He was a bright and multi-talented boy, with varied interests, and his parents were extremely proud of him. They wanted Viren to not only be perfect but ace everything. In their bid to push him to do better, Mr and Mrs Mathur never realised how much pressure they were putting on their son. Things reached such a head that one day Viren could not take it anymore. He ended his life because he didn't perform well in a preparatory paper for his 10th standard.

His death came as a blow to Tavish. He blamed himself for killing Viren because the day he hanged he had made sure to tie himself to the ceiling fan of his room in a way that anyone coming inside the room, would trigger the mechanism and the noose would tighten around his neck. And that someone happened to be Tavish. He walked into the room and froze, seeing Viren hanging by the ceiling fan. His body fidgeting in the last fatal seconds. His heart wanted to help him but his mind was blank. Before he could fathom what was happening and go to his brother's aid, Viren died in front of Tavish.

That night, sitting by the rugby field, Tavish bared his soul to Kisha, editing out some of the details. She couldn't sleep that night. She kept thinking of how Tavish must've coped with his brother's death. The guilt felt similar to the one she had within her. Had Kisha been here in Noida first, instead of Anara, the latter wouldn't have disappeared at all.

She also couldn't figure out why Tavish Mathur had shared such an intimate part of his life with her. They didn't even know each other properly. Was he comfortable with her? Did he think she would understand him? Or had she caught him in a weak moment? Would he have confessed this to any other person who had come to him at that time?

It was only during the wee hours of the morning that she arrived at the conclusion that perhaps he told her all that he did, because she was a ... stranger to him. The heartbreaking part, Kisha thought, was that maybe Tavish assumed they would remain strangers.

'May I ask you something?' Kisha asked, realising Tavish was about to turn and leave and that she did not want him to walk away just yet.

'Sure.'

'Do you think the heartbreak club is behind Anara's disappearance?'

Kisha saw a frown appear on Tavish's face.

'Two things: Who told you about the heartbreak club, really? And second, why do you think they were responsible for Anara's disappearance?'

Kisha made a decision within a second.

'Someone had anonymously messaged me that the Heartbreak Club is responsible for Anara di's disappearance.'

'Someone must have played a prank on you. And anyway, it's impossible to find out whether the club had a role in Anara's disappearance or not.'

'Why so?'

'All I know, or for that matter anyone in school knows, is that the Heartbreak Club is a secret club within the school. Nobody knows if it's even real. It's like Fairmont High's most infamous myth. And trust me, if the stories about them are true, nobody would want to rub them the wrong way. A lot has been attributed to them in the past decade. Never have they been busted. Not once in the twelve years of me studying here!'

'You mean the anonymous message was a hoax?'

'Most likely a prank as I said.' Tavish shrugged. He glanced at his watch and said, 'I think you have a class now.'

'Yes, captain.'

'Get going then. And don't overthink. A lot of shit has happened in Fairmont High. You don't want to open a Pandora's box, do you?'

Kisha found herself nodding, but her mind was telling her something else. Even her gut was in sync with her mind. The anonymous message wasn't a prank. Whoever sent it must know what the club was all about. But what's the point of sending her the message knowing she won't be able to do anything it? Something just didn't add up.

When Kisha reached her class, she noticed a roll of paper, loosely tied with a ribbon, on her desk. As she settled down and untied the ribbon, she realized it was a sketch. A closer look revealed that it was a reversible sketch. The kind where one side had an old toothless woman and the other showed the same girl, but as a queen. She was impressed. She turned the sketch but there was no signature. She looked around to see if she could guess who had kept the sketch there. She spotted him straight away. Ahaan Rawat was smiling at her shyly, looking at her from three rows behind her. Kisha gestured to him to ask if he had made the sketch. When he smiled and nodded happily, she mouthed a 'thank you' before the teacher came in. Once the class was over, she approached him.

'This is masterful, Ahaan. I didn't know you were this talented.'

Ahaan beamed from ear to ear. He said, 'I only show my talent to those whom I like.'

Wow, didn't expect him to be so forward. Flirt alert, was it? Kisha wondered and said, 'Amazing. I've to go now but again, thanks for this.' They exchanged another set of smiles. She felt Ahaan wanted to say something but he checked himself at the last moment. 'See you around,' he said.

'Sure.'

As Kisha went to the cycle stand, punched her code and unlocked her cycle, she noticed there was a note peeping out from under the seat. She took it out. A classic book's name was written on it. *The Catcher in the Rye.* Nothing else. *Is this THE note?* Kisha wondered and re-read the book's name. *What should I do with this? The obvious,* Kisha answered herself.

The library in Fairmont High International was open all round the clock. The librarians worked in shifts. When Kisha stepped into the library it was around ten at night. Except for the security outside and the librarian inside, there was nobody around. Kisha went to the series of desktop computers kept on the right side of the library entrance. It was basically a digital catalogue. Not only could a student track whether a book was in the library or not, but also know where exactly it was placed. Kisha sat by the chair and quickly typed the book's name on the search bar. *The Catcher in the Rye.* A coming of age classic, which Kisha had read at least three times. A long list opened up using which she could know how many times the book had been borrowed and by whom. One of the names she noticed in the list was of Anara Sen. Kisha moistened her dry lips and looked at its coordinates. S9, R10. S stood for shelf while R was for the row on the shelf.

Kisha rushed to the ninth shelf. Her eyes scanned the tenth row. There it was. Kisha took out the book and sat down on the adjacent bench. She opened the book with one question hovering on her mind: *What am I looking for?*

As Kisha flipped the pages, she noticed there were certain words highlighted on different pages. Kisha picked a pen and a small notebook from the table, and noted down the words in sequence as she discovered them highlighted in the book, till she was done with the book. The words on the paper stared at her: *If you want to be in the club, wear black nail polish tomorrow.*

A simple line but in it lay her invitation to join the Heartbreak Club. With a slight smile, Kisha put the bookmark back in the book, closed it and kept it on the shelf.

And then a thought popped into Kisha's head : *shit, I don't have a black nail polish.*

EIGHT

KISHA WORE BLACK NAIL POLISH DURING THE MORNING assembly the following day. It hadn't been that hard, getting her hands on it. She'd found it on the quick delivery app and hastily ordered it the night before. Now, standing in the morning assembly line, she felt like everyone was looking at her, though she also knew that was probably her own paranoia. Nobody really cared if she wore black nail polish, did they? And yet, she knew for sure she was being surveilled by the eyes of the Heartbreak Club members. What she hadn't anticipated were the other pair of eyes that spotted her while the assembly was dispersing.

'Wait a moment.' Dr Iyer's grim voice called out as she passed him with a nod of greeting.

Kisha immediately sensed that she was in trouble over the nail polish.

'Yes sir?' She turned and said in an innocently sweet voice.

'Who is your captain?'

In the next five minutes, Kisha found herself in the principal's room alongside Tavish.

'I didn't expect this from you Tavish. You're one of the brightest students we have. You didn't inform Miss Sen about the rules?' Dr Iyer sounded strict.

'I did, sir,' Tavish said and threw a glance at Kisha, his jaw clenched tight.

'He did, sir, he did,' Kisha said hastily. 'But I was a bit confused.'

'What do you mean?' Dr Iyer asked.

' As in, he told me cosmetics and jewellery aren't allowed. But he didn't exactly specify...'

' I see. And do we have to teach you, in standard eleventh, that nail polish comes under cosmetics?' Dr Iyer's tone was so neutral it was difficult to understand if he was being sarcastic or not.

'I'm sorry, sir,' Kisha said, realising it was better to apologise and close the matter than carry on a pointless argument.

'I suggest you review the rules once more. You two may leave now.'

Tavish stormed out of the principal's office with Kisha close on his heels.

'You know this could have affected my grades?' Tavish whirled around and said to Kisha, before she could present her apology to him. Kisha gulped. The truth was she hadn't actually thought about Tavish at all in her eagerness to break into the Heartbreak Club. He was right to be mad. None of this was his fault. She wondered if she should tell him why she wore the black polish in the first place.

'I hate it when people don't listen to me. Especially when I'm right. It just makes me feel someone else is controlling my stuff,' Tavish was saying, meanwhile. His anger seemed to ascend with the passing seconds.

'I get it. And I'm sorry but I had to wear the nail paint else—' for a fraction of a second Kisha hesitated. And then she blurted it out, 'I would have lost my only chance to get in touch with the heartbreak club.'

Tavish threw a flabbergasted look at her.

'I can't believe this. I told you not to get involved with them and yet here you are. You have no respect for your captain, isn't it? You have to pay the price then.' Tavish stood there thinking for some time.

'Okay, this is what we'll do. Get ten beer bottles to the boys' hostel tonight.'

Kisha thought she hadn't heard him correctly. Noticing the surprise on her face Tavish said, 'You heard that right. I've had enough of your drama.'

'But how will I get beer bottles? That too by tonight.'

'That's your problem. And I know you're smart enough to know the consequences if you don't do what you are being asked to.'

You'll report me to the principal for dissent. Kisha thought. 'Captain, please! You can't be so harsh,' Kisha began to say but Tavish turned his back on her and left. She understood that he was very angry and if she had to make things right with him, she'd have to do this task.

That evening, sitting in her room, Kisha had no clue how to get the bottles. She kept looking at her watch. There were only two hours left for her to get the bottles and deliver them to the boys' hostel. She thought of asking Vega for help, then decided it was too risky. Vega could very well trumpet it to the others. Moreover, Kisha had completely ignored Vega's proposal of talking her up to her crush. If she went to Vega, the girl would be on her case again about Tavish.

As Kisha mulled over her options, her phone pinged. It was Ahaan. *Hi, what's up?* the message read. Kisha responded. They exchanged a few messages and Kisha was surprised that Ahaan gauged that she wasn't being herself and asked for the reason. Kisha couldn't help but tell him about the bottles.

I can get the beer bottles, Ahaan replied.

How?

I know where the boys keep their hidden booze in the dorm. It's a secret but I know. And nobody will doubt me if I get them. You can give them their own bottles.

Kisha laughed at Ahaan's sneaky plan. He was much smarter than she had previously thought. Looks can sure be deceptive, she told herself.

You sure you can pull this off? What if you get caught? she typed.

Don't worry. I'll take it upon myself.

Why?

The reply came a little later: *Because.* A smiley followed it. Kisha wasn't stupid. She figured out Ahaan had a crush on her. But she decided to continue pretending like she was unaware of his affections. She certainly felt nothing romantic for him.

Exactly forty-five minutes later, Kisha met Ahaan near the under construction site of the new swimming pool. Rarely did any student go there and it almost always wore an abandoned look. Ahaan was carrying the bottles in a big duffel bag. He gave it to her and told her he would take it from her the next day. Kisha quickly thanked him and went straight to Tavish. She met him behind the boys' hostel.

'Wow. You actually managed. How did you—?'

'Is that part of the punishment? To answer how and where I got the bottles from?' said Kisha.

'Fair enough.' Tavish smirked and nodded. He looked around. There was no hostel security in sight. He took out one of the bottles, uncorked it with his mouth and spitting out the cork, gulped half the bottle down then and there. Then he took a deep breath and gulped more. Their eyes this time were locked as he finished the remaining beer. Neither blinked. Kisha felt his eyes were probing something within her. She had a funny feeling in her stomach that was making her uncomfortable. Should she say something? She didn't. With no further words, Tavish went around the hostel building, towards the entrance, with the bag. Kisha went back to the girls' hostel with a mission-accomplished-happy smile. Those eyes didn't leave her alone that night.

When Kisha woke up the next morning, she noticed she had ten missed calls from Tavish. She immediately called back but Tavish didn't answer. When she went to the canteen, Jas came up to her and said, 'Something tells me you don't know it yet.'

'What do I not know?' Kisha asked.

Jas took her phone out and showed her a video. It featured Tavish, taking out a beer bottle from a bag and uncorking it with his mouth. Then he took a big swig of beer and gulped it down. Kisha was shocked. This was from last night, she recognised the bag. This had happened after she had handed him the bottles. But the fact that she had been edited out of the video set her alarm bells ringing. It could very well appear to Tavish that it was her who had asked for the video to be recorded. Why else would she be edited out in such an obvious manner? As Kisha was collating her thoughts and wondering whether to message Tavish, she noticed Vega walk up to her.

'There has been a blunder.'

'I don't have time for your nonsense, Vega. This is serious—,' Kisha started to say.

'I recorded the video.'

'What! Why?'

'Because I wanted you to stay the hell away from Tavish. I told you he was mine.'

' It doesn't make sense. This video makes trouble for him, not me. Why didn't you record me?'

'My plan was to send him the video anonymously and insinuate that you recorded it but—'

'But?'

For the first time Kisha noticed some remorse on Vega's face. 'I don't know who leaked the video. That wasn't my plan at all. I never wanted to get Tavish into trouble. It wasn't me.'

'Then who did?'

'God knows. Now I'm afraid Tavish may have to bear the brunt of it.'

Kisha stood up and quickly went downstairs to her bike. As she cycled her way to the boys' hostel to meet Tavish, she saw him outside. Kisha braked hard, almost threw her bike to side of the road and ran to him.

'Tavish, I'm sorry for all this. Vega—'

'I know. I don't know who circulated it. But if I had known, I would have kissed the person for sure.'

Kisha looked at Tavish like he was mad. 'What?'

'I've been suspended for a week. And I've decided to go to the music fest that's happening in Delhi. The timing of this couldn't have been better. I really wanted to go but wasn't able to justify it to myself. But what is it they say? The universe …'

'Conspired to make it happen for you?' Kisha said and saw Tavish nod with pleasure. She'd never seen someone so jovial about their suspension. Feeling kind of zapped, she headed to the academic block for her classes.

It was during her class that she received a message on the school app. And more than the message what caught her attention was how the sender introduced himself.

Hey Kisha, I'm the Bishop of the Heartbreak Club.

NINE

WHY WOULD YOU DO THAT? KISHA TYPED FURIOUSLY. SHE had just been told that the video had been circulated by the Bishop.

Just wanted to sharpen my phone hacking skills, I guess? Hacked Vega's. The reply came swiftly. Kisha tried taking screenshot of the chat but the moment she did, a message popped up on the screen stating screenshots weren't allowed.

Nice try. Else I would have thought you're dumb.

Kisha felt like a fool but she still wanted to continue the conversation.

I really want to get in touch with you guys, she wrote.

She kept waiting, but there was no reply. After three minutes, the messages disappeared, dissolving the chat window. Kish gave a frustrated sigh.

Tavish returned to school, after his suspension, five days later. Nobody but Kisha knew he had actually made a little holiday of it. When the principal suspended him, he got a mail from Tavish's father expressing his disappointment at his son's behaviour and requesting that he be allowed to spend his suspension at home. Dr Iyer granted the permission not realising it was Tavish who had signed into his father's account and written that mail. On the first day of his suspension, Tavish hopped into a cab to Gurugram for the music fest. He stayed at a nearby budget hotel. The five days sped past. No pressure from parents. No need to ace anything. Just be; the most underestimated and under marketed concept.

'I have to tell you something,' Kisha said when she saw him on campus. She'd been thinking about it seriously for some time—if she wanted to figure out the Heartbreak Club quickly, she needed help. There was nobody she could talk to about it except Tavish. There were two reasons she felt she had to tell him. The first was he had been her sister's batchmate. If she told him about her plan, he might actually be able to give her some useful information. Also, for the plan that had started forming in her mind, Kisha knew she needed her captain to back her. Or else he would be a major roadblock later.

'Go on,' Tavish said. He seemed unusually relaxed, as if he had moved on from whatever had happened between them at the principal's office.

'Firstly, I'm sorry for the mess I created.'

'But why? You didn't record the video.'

'I know but the video was circulated partly because of me.'

'Really? And the other part?'

'Because someone from the Heartbreak Club has a twisted sense of fun.' Kisha took half a minute to tell Tavish about the messages she had received from the Bishop. Tavish heard her out in silence.

'I get it. You'll keep meddling with the club till either you figure them out or you cause yourself some harm.'

Kisha smiled taking it as a compliment.

'So, I might as well help you as much I can.'

Thank God he agreed, Kisha thought.

'Someone who called himself Bishop, chatted and told you he circulated the video for fun? Am I right?'

'That's correct. Though I'm not sure "Bishop" is a he.'

'Hmm, okay. Let's take a walk,' Tavish said and started walking away from the boys' hostel. Kisha understood he wanted to talk in private. A discussion on the Heartbreak Club was not for everyone's ears, she had understood this by now. As she caught up with him, she came straight to the point.

'I was thinking of talking to some of Anara's friends,' Kisha said looking at Tavish hopefully. So far, she had had no luck with any of Anara's classmates. No one seemed to want to talk to her.

Tavish threw a sharp glance at her and said, 'Do you even know who her friends were?'

'No. But I don't think it should be a problem for you.'

Tavish realised he had underestimated Kisha. The girl, after all, was a certified achiever. Of course, she had thought of everything. And was pinning her hopes on him to introduce her to Anara's friends and batch mates.

Tavish and Kisha had to attend classes for the day so they decided to meet again in the evening in the recreation room on campus. The room was full of indoor games for students. When Kisha entered, she noticed Tavish standing by the pool table with some other students. He looked at her, as she walked up to them.

'Guys, meet Kisha. She is Anara's younger sister.'

Reading the glances she got from the group, Kisha understood they already had that information. She waved to everyone. Tavish made the introductions.

'Demi.' *The girl with short hair.* Kisha smiled at her. As she met Anara's friends she wondered if any of them could have sent her the anonymous message to begin with. *Could it be Demi? Her confidence seemed uncompromised.*

'Selena.' *The girl with high-powered specs. Could it be her? Looks the intelligent type.*

'Mishal.' *The guy who is shorter than me. Him? Seems under confident and unsure.*

'So, Kisha, these were the people who were the closest to Anara. That's what I know, at least,' Tavish said.

'You know absolutely right. Anara was a part of us,' Demi said.

'Anything you guys want to share with me, which may help me understand why she went missing?'

There was a momentary pause as they exchanged looks. After that everyone started speaking almost at the same time.

'Anara never had any enemies so it's difficult to say if anyone was responsible for her disappearance,' Demi said. *Unless you were her enemy and nobody knew about it?* Kisha's mind was sprinting, shaping up possibilities.

'Nor was she unduly stressed about anything. Or else she would have told me at least. We were besties,' Selena said. *Maybe she did and that's why she vanished?*

'I think the police are right. She went away of her own free will.' Mishal sounded confident. *Maybe you are Mr Bullshit.*

'What if I were to tell you that the Heartbreak Club had a role to play in Anara di's disappearance?' Kisha said and observed the group go deathly silent.

'Generally, the victims of the club end up in an asylum. I haven't heard of anyone going missing so far,' Mishal said.

'Who ended up in an asylum? Anyone you know?' Kisha asked.

'Well, let me correct myself. Not all the victims. Also, I don't personally know them. But everyone in school knows about the Rajveer case. There were other cases too, but that's in the past. Like four or five years back. Rajveer is comparatively recent.'

'What's the Rajveer case?' Kisha asked. She noticed the others look around surreptitiously.

'Rajveer used to study here a couple of years back. He was a brilliant student, all set to go to an ivy league college. That was till the club hacked his computer, wrote an abusive SOP and sent it to the colleges on his behalf. Or at least that is what he said.'

'Shit!'

'Yeah. And he lost his mind over it. He had been preparing for it since he was in junior school. His life's goal was shattered. I think he is still in therapy.' Selena carried on from Mishal.

'Why would the club do that?'

'That's the thing,' Tavish said, taking a hit on the pool table. 'Nobody knows why they do what they do. What I've gathered over the years is they love forcing failures on students. Especially those whose heart is set on something.'

'Hence the name—the Heartbreak Club?'

'Maybe. I've studied in Fairmont High since a decade now. I've always known the club by this name.' Tavish shrugged.

'But how old is the club? I mean ... students can't be here forever?'

Mishal spoke up. 'Nobody said the club is made up of students. For all we know, it can be a club with teachers as well.'

Kisha swallowed a lump. This possibility had not occurred to her. The group slowly started to disperse. Kisha got up to leave when Selena signalled her to wait. After everyone else had left the room, Selena came to her and gestured that they walk out together.

'There's something which nobody knows. Except me. I mean, I never told this to anybody. Not even to the police who came here after Anara's disappearance,' Selena said, as they walked.

'What is it? And why didn't you tell the police?'

'I don't know. I felt it was personal and I wasn't sure how Anara would feel if I shared it. You see, Anara had a secret lover.'

'Oh! Any idea who it was?'

Selena shook her head. 'She never divulged a name. But she used to refer to the person as "she".'

It dawned on Kisha what Selena was hinting at. Could her elder sister be bisexual? Kisha thought. It wasn't a particularly disturbing revelation—one's sexual preference was one's own—but something definitely disturbed Kisha. She didn't know what exactly.

TEN

KISHA COULDN'T FOCUS ON HER STUDIES THAT NIGHT. *Anara had a girlfriend? Really?* Kisha knew her sister had quite a reputation in school, in London, for changing boyfriends faster than she changed clothes. But then, who enters into a lifelong commitment at that age anyway? Infatuations were common as were relationships that lasted a few weeks before fizzling out. Anara was hardly the only one going through boyfriends one after the other. Now, after what Selena had told her, Kisha wondered if Anara was exploring her sexuality. She had every right to do so, of course, but Kisha still found it a bit hard to believe. The reason was that Anara would usually tell her sister everything. But this had never come up, not even as a hint. Could the physical distance between them, once Anara moved to India, have caused a rift in their closeness? Was this something she wanted to meet and discuss? Kisha had to know and the only way to do it seemed to be to meet Rajveer. A solid link to the Heartbreak Club and an actual person whose life had been affected by them.

The next day was Sunday. Kisha obtained the necessary permission required to step out of campus from her father. She requested Tavish to join her in her plan. Tavish, besides being her captain, was a good ally to have, but truth be told, she also wanted him along because she liked his company. These days, Kisha found herself thinking of Tavish a lot. Sometimes she would close her eyes and his face would swim in front of her. His jawline especially was her weakness. Then the boys' locker scene which was a blush-trigger for her. Even while they spoke, she rarely managed to look at him straight. She didn't know if he had noticed it or not, but her eyes would wander to his jaw and then his mouth. One glance at his jawline and she would start getting butterflies in her stomach. Even the idea of his presence was enough for her to start knitting several emotionally arousing situations in her mind featuring both of them. He wasn't just a boy for her, but a spell.

Tavish was quick to agree to her plan to step out.

'It's Sunday and I'd do anything to avoid meeting my parents. So, let's go. I'll tell them I have extra classes and they shouldn't visit, while I would mail the principal from my dad's email id for a permission,' he said. Together they left school. It hadn't been difficult to trace Rajveer's address. Tavish had messaged one of his seniors on Instagram, who had passed out a year after Rajveer's batch. He, in turn, connected him to another boy who was a family friend of Rajveer's. And so, the address was secured. A bungalow near HUDA City Centre, in Gurugram.

A person's house says a lot about him. And Rajveer's house shouted to the world that he was from a supremely wealthy family. As Kisha and Tavish entered the hall of the huge bungalow, a couple of friendly golden retrievers ran up to them and sniffed around. Kisha petted them, reminded of Fluff, who she had left behind in London.

The boy who had shared Rajveer's address had shared his number as well. Tavish had called Rajveer and let him know that he and Kisha were coming over to meet him. Mindful of his mental state he didn't want to spring a surprise on him. Luckily, Rajveer had agreed to meet them. Yet, when he walked into the living area, Tavish and Kisha were taken aback. Though Rajveer was older than them, he looked a school kid. He was frail and there was a jumpiness about him. He came and sat opposite them.

'So, what's this about?'

'Hi Rajveer, this is Kisha. I'm Tavish. Her captain in Fairmont High.'

A smile touched Rajveer's face. 'Good old days.'

'Rajveer, my sister Anara is missing for the past eight months. And I believe the Heartbreak Club is responsible,' Kisha said, unable to stop herself. Rajveer's face changed. Kisha realised she shouldn't have thrown that name so early and bluntly in front of him. He looked troubled, as if he was in a lot of pain that he was trying to suppress.

'Do you guys know anything about me?' Rajveer asked. His tone was cold.

Both Tavish and Kisha nodded.

'Thought so. It's good you came when my parents aren't here or else they wouldn't have let you meet me. You know, it's been more than a year and I still have to visit the shrink once every week.'

There was silence. Kisha wasn't sure how to direct the conversation back to Anara and the Heartbreak Club.

'They wanted me to be a part of them. They'd offered me their black handshake, their initiation rite to enter the club. I don't know who they were exactly. I had heard about the club in school but no one said anything much. All I knew was that they were a super secretive club. They used to communicate with me using classic book titles with highlighted texts.'

Kisha's heart skipped a beat. This was exactly what was happening with her as well. It meant she was actually dealing with the club people.

'The members have specific designations—king, queen, knight, bishop, rook and pawn. They wanted me to be their pawn at that point,' Rajveer continued.

Kisha moistened her lips nervously. The Bishop had reached out to her. The dots were slowly connecting. Tavish noticed her nervousness but pretended to be focused on Rajveer.

'If you guys are here to know more about the club, then I am sorry, that's all I know. I don't have more information. If I did, I would have nailed those bastards by now.' Pent up anger raised its ugly head as he spat out those words.

'Why did you not join them as a pawn?' Kisha asked.

'Because I didn't want to. They told me they believe in breaking people's confidence, their hearts. If one had a passion that lit up their soul, they would extinguish it. They had some twisted logic. To give students a taste of supreme emotional failure. Make them "date" darkness. Pull them down to ground zero. It's their way of injecting the "fight" in you. They say those who get up after getting their heart broken in this way, are the ones who make it big in life eventually. If a student dreams, or falls in love, or puts their heart and soul into something, the Heartbreak Club decides whether that dream lives or dies. Whether the *heart* to put into something even survives. They expose a student's deep-seated weakness. They keep their clout in school by rubbing authority the wrong way,' Rajveer spoke without a pause, as if a tap had been opened. A thoughtful pause later he added, 'Well, they did make me date darkness. Jokers.'

'Who told you all this?' Kisha asked.

'The Heartbreak Club did. These were messages sent to me, highlighted in books. The names of the books used to be messaged to me.'

'What a weird way to think. Since they are so confident about their process, did they have any success stories?' Kisha looked intrigued.

'There were a few, I guess. I had heard of this student whose heart was into cricket. They destroyed his love for the game by attacking his reputation falsely and making sure he doesn't get selected in any team. But after that, the student's will to prove himself was inflamed. He became even better at the sport. So much so that he is playing for an IPL franchise currently.'

'That's correct, I know this story. Saurav Gupta. He plays from the Delhi team in IPL,' Tavish said.

'There you go.' Rajveer looked at both Tavish and Kisha alternately.

Kisha was about to ask Rajveer another question when she noticed how he was shaking his legs. He suddenly stood up and left the room. Tavish and Kisha looked at each other blankly. A man, presumably, came in after a minute and told them Rajveer had retired for the day and that they should leave. The two got up, realising this was all they would get from him.

'Coffee?' Tavish asked the moment they had stepped out of Rajveer's house. In the next hour, Kisha found herself sitting opposite her captain in a cafe. While he was ordering, looking up at the waiter, Kisha stared at his profile. There it was, the jawline. Normally, she would have avoided looking at him so blatantly, but in that moment, she couldn't help it. And when

Tavish turned to ask her what she would have, for a second she went blank before snapping back to reality and ordering a frappe. As the waiter went away, Kisha smiled at Tavish. They had never spent time outside of the school premises and she wasn't sure of how to behave with him. Was he her captain even outside the school? Should she maintain the formality or could she be a little casual with him?

'So,' Tavish began. 'Any difference between India and the UK? I mean I'm sure there is but what's your take on it?'

'I find people here are less spiteful. The students I've come across this far, at least.'

'And yet it's here that your sister went missing.'

'I know. But such things do happen in the UK too. Anyway, comparisons are pointless.' Kisha wanted to steer the conversation towards a different direction. She asked, 'You tell me, captain, what else is up except school?'

'Nothing really. Are you asking about anything specific?'

'Any girlfriend?'

She noticed a faint smile on his face. He shook his head.

'None?' Kisha sounded surprised.

'None right now. A couple in the past, but it didn't work out.'

'Why? If I may know.'

'That is privileged information. And I would like any girl, who wants to know why, to get in to a relationship with me and earn the right to find out.'

Whoa, Kisha thought. He is flirting with me but in a way that I can't even pin point. There's a proposition in his statement and yet… Kisha shifted in her seat.

'No comeback?' Tavish asked.

'Just wondering...'

'What about?'

How it would be to be in a relationship with you, Kisha thought, but said aloud, 'Do you believe in it?'

'Believe in what?'

'A person is different when single and different in a relationship. Do you believe that?'

'Depends. I think sometimes in order to appease the one we love, we end up becoming someone else. For better or for worse.'

That's surely coming from experience, Kisha thought. Something that she didn't have. Kisha was not only a virgin but she hadn't even kissed a boy yet. It wasn't because she was a prude but the boys, she always believed, were reserved for her elder sister. Nobody ever approached her in London. Maybe because she was an achiever, boys were intimidated by her. Her IQ was higher than the sharpness of their inherent male egos. And no boy she knew was secure enough to date a girl who was famous.

The chit chat over coffee gave Kisha a glimpse of the person that Tavish was. When he had told her about the impact his twin's death had on him, she knew he was sensitive. Inferring from what he said about his two relationship—it didn't work out—means somewhere they were serious. It was safe for her to believe he wasn't into casual dating even though that was what was expected from a boy of his age. This reminded her of a line Anara had told Kisha once.

'Deep people rarely date casually.'

'Then why are you dating different guys all the time?' Kisha had shot back.

'I'm trying to understand my depth,' Anara had said with a serious face and burst out laughing mischievously.

So, was Tavish deep or in the trying-to-figure-the-depth phase?

'What kind of girls do you like?' Kisha asked.

'I don't have a set pattern in head. Everyone's different. And there lies the magic. Do you have a generalisation of the kind of boys you like?'

'Umm, I do have some basic red flags.'

'Like?'

'I hate abuse. Mental-physical-emotional. Any kind.'

'I too have a red flag.' Tavish noticed Kisha's curious face and continued, 'I don't like those who get into a relationship with a let's-see-where-it-goes kind of vibe. I'm more about destinations. Whether we reach the destination or not is a different story. But sorry, I can't float in the air with anyone. I should know from day one what's mine, how much of what's mine is mine and why that's so.'

Kisha swallowed a small lump since Tavish just mirrored what she felt about relationships. She noticed Tavish leave the coffee mid-way and order a cold drink.

'You just had a hot coffee,' Kisha said.

'So? I want to have something cold. I go by feeling and not what I'm supposed to or not supposed to do.'

Looking at Tavish making the payment for the cold drink, she concluded that he was surely temperamental. He glanced at her next and said, 'You know I hate cafes.'

'Then why here?' a perplexed Kisha asked.

'It's good to go against your likes and visit places you hate, sometimes. Just so you know more about yourself. Love, maybe, is a teacher but hate … it's a professor. Gives you more advance knowledge.'

And he is a contradiction as well. But somewhere that

contradiction seemed alluring to Kisha. And he was interesting. The fact that she never knew how he was going to answer her many questions, made conversation intriguing.

'I didn't ask but what was your take on Anara di?' Kisha asked. The sudden mention of Anara took Tavish by surprise. He took few seconds to collate his thoughts.

'She was so promising. Like whatever she did, she did it with utmost passion. Anara was the in-it-to-win-it kind. But honestly, I never got to know her personally much. We were batch mates, sure, but I guess I was still getting to know her before she …'

He didn't have to complete the rest.

It was evening by the time they returned to the school premises. After coming back to her room, she video called Ranya. Her mother was out as well. They conversed for some time until she noticed a message from Ahaan on her WhatsApp. It read: *I'm waiting outside the girls' hostel. Can we please meet?* With a frown Kisha ended the call with her mother and grabbed her jacket. She noticed Ahaan the moment she came out of the hostel.

'Hey Kisha,' he said with a shy smile.

'Hey Ahaan. Is everything okay? What happened?'

'Nothing. Just wanted to see you.'

'See me? I didn't get you.'

'I wanted to see you, Kisha.'

'But why?'

'I don't know. I just felt like it.'

The entire conversation didn't make any sense to Kisha. *Is it just because he has a crush on me which is scribbled all over his face but he doesn't have the balls to tell me? So, he will try these weird acts?* Kisha wondered. Perhaps this was the reason why nobody ever befriended him in class. Kisha knew he was the quiet type but she didn't know he had zero social sense. She thought it would be best to terminate the conversation.

'Fine, I guess you've seen me now,' Kisha said before turning to leave.

'Wait, Kisha,' Ahaan said and stopped her.

'What's going, Ahaan?' Kisha said looking at him.

Ahaan took out something from the bag he was carrying. Kisha immediately knew what it was. A sketch. Ahaan presented it to her. It was a sketch of a deity with ten hands except the face was Kisha's. Being a Bengali, Kisha immediately knew which Goddess it was. But what was the point? Kisha was confused. Was this guy telling her that he was devoted to her? Did he worship her? Kisha felt the creeps even thinking about it. The sketch was excellent but the attention was unwanted. He was coming on to her too strongly.

'Thanks, Ahaan, but I can't take this,' Kisha said. She knew she was being firm but she believed being upfront was the best way to deal with the situation. She saw Ahaan's face fall.

'But why? I made it for you.'

'Yes, but I didn't ask you to. And I don't want to accept it, so, please.' Kisha turned and walked away.

Vega saw Kisha walk away while Ahaan stood, looking crestfallen. She glanced at her phone. She had managed to click the two together right before Kisha had left. It looked like Kisha and Ahaan were in deep conversation.

Earlier that morning, she'd seen Kisha and Tavish leave the school together. She kept an eye on the school gate and sure enough the two returned in the evening, talking and laughing together. It singed Vega to see them, for she had had a crush on Tavish for the longest time. She had even asked him out a couple of times in the past three years, always to be refused gently. Vega had held on to the hope that if she eliminated any possible competition, Tavish would be with her one day. By now she had also understood Kisha would never talk her up to Tavish. She was eyeing him herself. Vega immediately shared the picture with Tavish on WhatsApp with a message: *Am I not as talented as Kisha?* She was confident Tavish would know what she meant. A bitchy smile touched her face.

As soon as Tavish received the photo from Vega, he felt a furious rage. A nerd like Ahaan was approaching Kisha, someone for whom he had started developing feelings, though it was something he had only just realised.

The next morning, when Kisha was about to enter her class, Jas came running to her. Her face was flushed with excitement. Jas, as Kisha knew by now, was the school news keeper. She was like the human twitter, collating the latest happenings and then getting everyone's opinion about it. Jas gave Kisha a breathless account of the fight in the boys' hostel. She told Kisha that Tavish had threatened Ahaan for approaching her. What made Kisha smile was the last thing Jas told her before they entered the class.

'Everyone heard Tavish say that you were his girl. So, everyone's now curious if you guys are actually in a relationship.' Jas' excitement was pronounced.

Kisha wanted to ask more but the class had started by then.

She sat down but focus was a far cry. She kept thinking of the time she spent in the café with Tavish and wondered if he too had started feeling for her the way she did. *She is my girl ...* she was craving to hear it from him.

After class, she looked for her captain everywhere. Finally, she found him in the rugby field, practising with a few boys. She ran to him and stood beside him, catching her breath. He looked at her but didn't say anything. *Did he know, I would come to him?*

'Let me guess, news of me threatening Ahaan must have reached you. Of course, I would never beat him or anyone who doesn't match me. He just had to be warned. And warn him I did. But you are here to ask why I did it.'

No, I want to hear what you said there. That I'm your girl.
'Kind of,' Kisha said. Tavish stood right in front of her. He gave her a quick peck on her cheek. Kisha stood frozen. The other boys had turned their backs to them. Tavish went ahead to join them. Kisha's eyes were registering the fact that Tavish was walking away from her but she couldn't say anything. As if she didn't know any language. And standing there, feeling his lips on her cheek still, rattling her soul, Kisha for the first time understood why action was given more importance than words.

ELEVEN

STRANGELY ENOUGH, NEITHER TAVISH NOR KISHA BROUGHT up the peck. It was as if both understood that it was meant to be an unspoken secret between them. And thus, it remained so. The week after that was the school's music competition. The competitions were for solo performances as well as duets. Kisha went to sign herself up for the piano competition. While waiting around, she noticed her name already listed for one of the duet rounds. With Tavish. He hadn't even asked her, but she was to play her piano alongside his electric guitar. It was something new for her, and exciting. Both, the competition as well as what she was feeling for Tavish.

Even though they didn't talk about their moment on the rugby field, Kisha knew something had changed between them. She noticed some changes within her, as well as in Tavish. For instance, she started taking note of how many girls approached Tavish to talk and flirt. When she wasn't with him she used to wonder if he was talking to any of them. It was both funny and weird. As for Tavish, she had noticed that whenever some boy approached her, even if it was for the smallest of things, Tavish's eyes would be on her, trying to appear casual and failing. The fact that she was under his watch, aroused her emotionally. Never before had someone made her conscious of her own actions in such a beautiful way. As if everything she did meant something to someone. As if even her most mundane actions were special because someone was noticing it.

And then there were the music rehearsals where she would sit behind the piano, her fingers gliding on the keys, while Tavish would strum the electric guitar, his eyes never leaving her. He said the rehearsals were for them to build a rapport and rhythm, and it did. Just not the kind he meant. It was of her eyes getting used to her fast heartbeats whenever his eyes were on hers. A different music was being played within them which only they could hear. On the day of the competition, they stood second in the duet round while Kisha won the solo level.

After she was handed the trophy, Kisha went backstage. She found Tavish waiting for her with something which used to kill her softly; his smile.

'Congrats, Kish,' he said. 'Kish' from Kisha was also a change that had happened after the peck. She quite liked it, though she never commented on it. In fact, she acted like she had not even noticed the change. She saw Tavish take out something from his pocket. It was a small owl pendant with two evil eyes where it's eyes should've been.

'This is for you.'

'Wow, this is so amazing,' Kisha said.

'This was my brother's.'

Kisha's smile froze.

'Then it must be precious.'

'It is. I was waiting to gift this to someone.'

'And you chose me?' Kisha sounded more surprised than she was.

'You met my criteria.'

'And that was?'

Tavish came close to her. The knot in Kisha's stomach tightened. Never had he stood this close to her with other students and staff around.

'That I should love the person as much as I loved my brother.' His warm breath on her skin gave her gooseflesh and a funny feeling in her stomach. The intimacy of his presence was so intense that she wanted to take a step back. She stood her ground though.

Their eyes lingered for just that extra second, the truth about their feelings burning between them. Then Tavish abruptly turned and walked away. She stood tongue-tied with the pendant in her hand. Other students came up and congratulated her but Kisha barely paid attention. She seemed far away, still thinking about the moment when Tavish's breath hit her ears while he whispered to her. He had kept the evil eye for someone he loved as much as his brother ... for someone he loved ... he loved. It was a proposal. She couldn't have misinterpreted it. But in a proposal, one proposes and the other either accepts or rejects. Did Tavish know she'd accepted him already?

After the euphoria of the music competition had died down, she went to the Wall of Dedication. It was a massive wall by the assembly hall, on which students wrote messages and dedications. The wall was already full and new dedications had to be scribbled over old ones. Kisha decided to dedicate her win to Tavish.

'To the one who frees me. O Captain, my captain.' She wrote and smiled. She ran her eyes over a few dedications. A name sprang out at her: Anara! Kisha peered closely, trying to figure out what Anara had written. Already people had scribbled over it. Finally, she could make out the words: 'I love my Tiger.' Kisha clicked a picture of it with her phone.

Who was 'Tiger'? Kisha wondered, but nobody came to mind. Anara had loved someone by the name of Tiger? Or had she nicknamed this person 'Tiger'? But didn't she have a girlfriend? But tigers were male. Or had she written 'Tigress'? No, it was definitely 'Tiger'.

During dinner, Kisha was sitting with Jas, eating her food, when Selena came and sat opposite her.

'How are you doing?' Selena asked.

'Good. You?' Kisha said.

Selena kept chitchatting about this and that, while Kisha wondered what her real reason for sitting there was. Just then, Jas excused herself to get some more rice. Selena quickly put a paper napkin under Kisha's plate. 'Read it when you are alone,' she said in a low tone.

'Do you know someone by the name of Tiger?' Kisha asked before Selena could leave. The girl's face told her she was unprepared for it. The next second, she shrugged, shook her head and left.

Jas came back and settled down to eat. Kisha was bursting with curiosity. Knowing that Selena was Anara's close friend, she had a hunch that the note would be about her sister. Before Jas could stop her, or ask any questions, Kisha lifted her plate along with the paper napkin, and excused herself.

Kisha kept the food tray on the side of the counter where the used plates were stacked. Clasping the napkin tightly, she went towards the washroom. Once inside, Kisha took out the napkin and read. The message was clear: *Meet me by the under-construction swimming pool. Important. Destroy this after reading.* Kisha scrunched the napkin and threw it in the toilet bowl. As she flushed it, Kisha wondered about all the secrecy. Some new information about Anara was about to be revealed, she was sure of it. She could feel her heart suddenly beat faster.

In the next minute, Kisha was walking towards the under construction swimming pool area. She had thought about taking her cycle but then decided against it. The app-based cycles kept a log of who had taken a bike and up to where. Kisha figured if Selena had gone through so much secrecy, she may not want to keep a record of where they were meeting.

As Kisha headed towards the meeting spot, not for a second did she realise that she was being followed by Vega. When she had seen Kisha give up her dinner half way and rush to the washroom, Vega had got suspicious. She was still annoyed about how her past plan to malign Kisha to Tavish had failed. Now, she followed the new girl, taking care to stay in the shadows, in the hope that she would be able to collect some incriminating evidence against her. Vega saw Kisha climb into the emptied out swimming pool. She stopped wondering what to do next. There was no light in the area since the place was closed off to students. The only lighting was from some distant reflections.

Suddenly Vega saw a shadowy figure leap out of nowhere and rush towards Kisha from behind.

'Kisha! Look out!' Vega screamed.

By then Kisha had been hit on her shoulder. But the shadowy figure also fumbled, taken aback at hearing Vega's voice. It ran away, disappearing into the darkness. Vega scampered towards Kisha, who was clutching her shoulder, her eyes squeezed tight. The excruciating pain she was in, made her miss the obvious: that Vega was not supposed to be there.

'Don't worry, Kisha. Just hold me tight. Let's take you to the hostel,' Vega said. Still in shock, Kisha accompanied Vega slowly. As they neared the premises, Ahaan came running towards them.

'What happened to her?'

Vega glanced at Ahaan, then at Kisha. She wasn't sure how much Kisha wanted to divulge.

'Nothing. I fell down,' said Kisha and kept walking.

Vega took Kisha to her room and called the on-campus doctor. He checked Kisha and, after making sure no bones were broken, gave her a pain killer and asked her to rest. When she woke up the next day, Kisha felt the pain had subsided considerably. She checked her phone. There were fifteen missed calls from Tavish. She called him.

'What happened to you?' he asked. The fact that he picked the call within two rings told Kisha he had been worried. And waiting. His intention behind the worry turned her on despite the pain she was in.

'I think I was attacked by the Heartbreak Club.'

'What?'

'Selena had called me to the under-construction swimming pool to discuss something important. There I was attacked.'

'Are you okay? I can involve the principal if you want to take action against Selena.'

Kisha was flattered by the restlessness she could sense in Tavish. It was a sign of how much he cared for her. But she had to calm him down at that point.

'Relax. I am fine and I'll talk to Selena myself. I was thinking why THC didn't approach me even when I did what they'd asked me to do. Wear the black nail polish. Maybe it was just a silly prank. And this attack was to scare me away. But now I have a plan for the Heartbreak Club.'

'What's the plan?'

'I'll tell you but first, please come and meet me. I ... I'm missing you, captain,' Kisha said. There was silence for a few seconds after which Tavish said, 'Will be right there.'

THE HEARTBREAK CLUB: CHAT FILES – 2

THE CHAT WINDOW POPPED UP ON THE SCHOOL APP. PEOPLE joined immediately.

KING: Why wasn't Vega's presence noted when Kisha was being attacked?

BISHOP: Sorry, King. Even though I attacked Kisha but I totally missed Vega.

KNIGHT: I hope the attack puts some sense into Kisha.

PAWN: She did wear the black nail polish. When do we give her the black handshake, her test to enter THC?

KING: We were toying with her. We give her the black handshake only if she still persists with trying to find more about us after this attack. Till then we lie low. Also, let's all be careful as well. This negligence about Vega wasn't good. We have to be more careful than ever. Never before in the history of this club has anybody ... died.

PAWN: Understood.

KNIGHT: Understood.

BISHOP: Understood.

ROOK: Understood.

BISHOP: Is Queen dead? She hasn't joined any meet for a while now.

A deafening silence followed.

KING: Didn't I mention during our earlier chat that I'll see what Queen's up to? I know where Queen is. There shouldn't be any more questions on that.

BISHOP: Sorry, King.

PAWN: Just one question, King. May I?

KING: Shoot.

PAWN: Why did we give her the black handshake if we were going to attack her?

KING: So that Kisha understands that the black handshake was a prank but the attack was real. Hopefully, she'll back out, sensing how dark things can get from here on. Anything else?

Nobody messaged.

KING: Dissolve. Now!

The members left the chat room one after another and the chat room disappeared to where it had come from.

TWELVE

'I'M SO SORRY. BELIEVE ME, I HAD NO IDEA SOMETHING like this could happen. I wanted to speak to you in complete secrecy and so I asked you to come to the pool. Had the warden not stopped me, while I was heading towards the pool, I would have actually reached before you. But how anyone else found out, I will never know,' Selena said when she went to meet Kisha in the music room. Kisha was feeling a little chaotic in her mind. And whenever she felt that way, music became her healer.

'I understand. It's not your fault. Anyway, what was it that you wanted to tell me?'

Selena looked around. There were a few students there, tinkering with instruments. Nobody seemed interested in them.

'I told you Anara had a secret girlfriend, right?'

Kisha nodded, staring keenly at Selena.

'The reason I knew about the secret girlfriend was because it was me,' Selena said. Kisha didn't know how to react exactly.

'Since you were her girlfriend, you would know if something was bothering her, wouldn't you?'

Selena thought for some time and said, 'Nothing that I can recollect.'

'Don't you think it's weird that a normal, healthy girl suddenly disappeared?'

Selena took her time to speak. When she did, Kisha's hand trembled hearing her.

'Maybe she hasn't disappeared. Maybe she's been killed,' Selena said quietly.

'What! What makes you think so?'

'The Heartbreak Club. You said they were behind her disappearance. They are capable of anything.'

'But have they ever killed before?' Kisha asked. Selena's silence was her answer.

'Anything else I should know?'

'No, I'm afraid. I just wasn't able to live in peace without telling you the truth. Anara and I were in a relationship and it felt like an important detail. Something her sister should know. But please don't make this public. I don't want to—'

'I would never do such a thing. Tell me, do you know any Tiger? Or do you know if Anara knew someone called Tiger?'

'Tiger? No, why?'

'Nothing. Thanks, Selena for opening up to me like this. It means a lot.'

'It's the least I could have done. But I haven't told this to the police either. I hope you will keep my secret.'

'Don't worry. Tell me something, is it possible the club members may have manipulated the situation in a way that the warden reached you when you were coming to meet me?' Kisha asked.

Selena thought for a moment and said, 'I wish I could completely reject this theory but it's possible. And…' a thought seemed to cross her mind. 'OMG, maybe they did this so you would think I'm part of THC?'

Kisha knew Selena had a point. There was nothing more to ask.

Selena left. Kisha turned towards her piano but she couldn't play it. She was too distracted by whatever Selena had told her, besides her shoulder still hurt. In between classes, she went to look for Tavish. She knew it was time for his rugby practice and she would find him on the field. The same place where his lips had touched her skin for the first time. Kisha was thinking back to their kiss when Tavish came running to her, leaving the game mid-way.

'Hey! How are you feeling now?'

'Much better,' Kisha said. The concern in his voice pleased her immensely.

'If I could only figure out who attacked you and why, I can guarantee you they wouldn't dare do this to anyone else. Unfortunately, I can't think of anyone. But you said you'd a plan, right?'

'I do. When you seek something and it doesn't come to you, it's better to stop and let the thing seek you.'

'Okay, but can you cut the Rumi out and tell me in a normal way what you have in mind?'

Kisha laughed and told him her plan. Hearing it Tavish smiled giving her an incredulous look.

'I thought your eyes were the sexiest thing about you,' Tavish said and then, holding her head, added, 'And now you introduced me to your brain, gosh.' Kisha had gooseflesh everywhere.

From that very evening, Kisha and Tavish started executing their plan. The two slunk around campus, looking for empty spots. While one of them kept watch, the other took out a spray paint can. On went the paint on the walls—*It's THC who is responsible – ANARA.*

By morning, the news had not only reached every student in Fairmont High but also every staff member. During the assembly, Dr Iyer decided to address the issue.

'Students, I've been told, and have seen myself too, that some disturbing graffiti has come up in the school premises. Someone is pretending to write from the perspective of a missing student. The issue the graffiti is highlighting is already a police case. I haven't yet informed the police because our school has some prestige in the world outside and things like this don't create a good impression. I've ordered for the removal of the graffiti with immediate effect. And if I see any again, I would be compelled to bring in the police. Thank you.'

The only people whose faces fell were Kisha and Tavish. Their plan was squashed even before it could bear any result. Or so they feared. After classes, sitting alone in the rugby field they discussed if they should pursue the club further or just leave it.

'You know, if I didn't have the guilt I would have perhaps let go, assuming it's all a waste anyway. I mean, mom and dad have. But this guilt—'

'Why guilt?'

Kisha moistened her lips and told Tavish that one thing which she had carried in her heart since she came to know Anara was missing.

'Anara di was never supposed to be here. It was me. But because I was in rehab, Anara di came here. I feel like we swapped our destinies ...'

Tavish remained quiet. Kisha was expecting him to say something—either console her or ask her more, but he was silent. It felt therapeutic to finally share her innermost thoughts with someone who didn't inundate her with questions. She understood the value of someone who knew how to cover one's wounds with silence. A little later Tavish confided in her about his own guilt about his brother. How he blamed himself for not knowing what hell he was going through while he was alive.

Opposites may attract, Kisha thought, *but people with similar wounds belong together.*

Deciding that they would let the pursuance of the heartbreak club be for a while, Tavish and Kisha walked up to her cycle which she'd parked right outside the rugby field. During their walk across the field, Tavish kept wondering if he should tell Kisha that Anara was once trying to woo him but looking at her, and knowing how much she was in love with him, Tavish decided otherwise. Confessing the truth wasn't enough, sometimes the timing of the confession was important. He decided to let the confession be. It wouldn't have added anything to her search for Anara. Instead, it could lead to a hiccup in their blooming love story. They reached Kisha's parked cycle.

They both noticed a paper note, fluttering in the wind, stuck into the handle bar. On it was the name of a classic book, along with the coordinates of where it was in the library. They exchanged a startled glance. Both knew where the note must've come from. And both rushed to the library together leaving the cycle behind.

THIRTEEN

KISHA AND TAVISH CAME INTO THE LIBRARY, HUFFING and puffing. They checked the note again and ran towards the shelf it mentioned. There was no one around, just the librarian who was sitting and reading, what looked like, a well-thumbed romance. She eyed the two with a raised eyebrow. The library wasn't a place where anyone showed any urgency. Kisha forced a smile at the librarian, while Tavish didn't care. He reached the shelf first. By the time Kisha came up, he had taken out the book mentioned in the note as w ell.

'Now what?' he asked. Kisha remembered how she had read the message in the book the last time. She took the book from Tavish and flipped through it. Soon she spotted words which were highlighted. Just like they were the last time.

'I'll read out the words, you make a note,' she said. Tavish quickly ran to the librarian and got a pen and a notepad. They got to work. When they were done, they sat down and studied the words. After arranging them in a few different ways, they eventually arrived on a sentence that made sense. What it said blew their minds.

If you want to be in, make the one who issued this book last fall in love with you and break his heart in such a way that he is deeply damaged. That's our black handshake for you.

'Black handshake?' Kisha muttered under her breath.

'That's what the Heartbreak Club call their initiation rite. Rajveer had told us, remember?' Tavish said. Kisha did remember. She closed the book and remained thoughtful for some time.

'So, our graffiti plan worked in a way,' she said after a pause.

'Looks like it. But do we believe in it whole heartedly? How can we be sure this isn't a prank?' They were talking in whispers.

Kisha knew Tavish had a point.

'Should we find out who checked out the book from the library last?' she asked.

'That's the way to go.'

They went to the librarian with the book.

'Good afternoon, ma'am,' said Kisha sweetly. 'We were wondering if you could tell us who issued this book last?'

'Why?' said the librarian, eyeing them both suspiciously.

Kisha and Tavish shared a quick glance.

'We noticed that some words in the book are highlighted. So, we thought of checking,' Tavish said.

'Highlighted? What do you mean? Let me see.'

The librarian took the book, flipped the pages and realised Tavish was right.

'But this was clean. I had seen it when I took it from ...' she said, while checking her desktop computer. Tavish and Kisha exchanged a look. They were very close to finding out who had issued the book last. But when the librarian read the name aloud, both looked zapped.

'Ahaan Rawat. Standard XI A.'

Of course, it's the same weirdo I know, Kisha thought as she rolled her eyes.

'It has to be a prank,' Tavish muttered under his breath, loud enough for Kisha to understand what he said.

They thanked the librarian and left. The two quietly walked out of the building, a tense silence between them. Kisha could sense Tavish didn't like what they had discovered. But before she could say anything, he spoke up.

'I am not convinced. It may well be possible that Ahaan, knowing you are after THC, set this whole thing up only so you give him attention,' he said. Kisha couldn't deny it completely. The idea had crossed her mind too. It couldn't be a coincidence that people from the Heartbreak Club wanted her to woo the same guy who had been trying to get into her radar all this while. Unless...

'Or maybe THC knows I'm way out of Ahaan's league. Not being a snob but you know what I mean. And hence they want me to do what I wouldn't have done normally. Like if they had mentioned your name, then it would be easy for me. From whatever I understood of what Rajveer told us, these THC people are sadists.'

Tavish knew Kisha was right.

'Could be true but I want to cross-check this Ahaan bit once,' Tavish said.

'How?'

'I have my ways.'

'No violence please, Tavish.'

'Nobody will get hurt, is what I can promise.'

Kisha liked the fact that Tavish didn't debate with her on that point.

'I want to know if any student dropped out in the last few years because they were deeply damaged emotionally,' said Kisha.

'Rajveer did.'

'Anyone else? You've been here longer than I have. You must've heard stories,' Kisha said. Tavish thought hard.

'I don't remember the name but a girl did drop out. I remember she tried to take her life. This happened two years before Rajveer. Wait a minute, even a boy from our batch last year, Namashi, had the same fate. Gosh, I didn't know these could be connected to THC.'

'I don't think we can reach out to them, can we? Like we reached out to Rajveer?' Kisha asked.

Tavish shook his head. 'Firstly, neither were from Delhi. Secondly, do we even have that much time to wait till Sunday?'

'Does that mean...' Kisha was about to complete her sentence when Tavish cut her short saying, 'First let me figure out Ahaan's ass.'

'Just don't kick his ass,' Kisha said, gave a quick peck on his cheeks and cycled towards the girls' hostel without even waiting to check Tavish's reaction.

That night in the boys' hostel, Tavish, his close friend Surya and a couple of other guys barged into Ahaan's room. While his friends cornered Ahaan, Tavish started searching the room for any possible clues that could say either he was a THC member or was toying with Kisha. An hour later Tavish got nothing. Zilch. He went to Ahaan and, holding him by his collar, said, 'If it was not for Kisha I would have broken all your teeth. But listen carefully. If I get to know you are toying with Kisha in any way, you will have hell to pay.'

'I'm up to nothing of that sort. Trust me.'

Tavish hated it but he read genuineness in Ahaan's eyes under his fear.

'You better not be,' Tavish said and then he and his friends left the room. Ahaan immediately messaged Kisha.

Kisha was having dinner when she received the text: *Is everything alright? Tavish came to my room looking for something.*

Kisha didn't reply. She knew if Tavish had got something he would have called her immediately. She knew now the decision would have to be made. If, for a moment, she considered that the real Heartbreak Club had sent out the proposal of allowing her a chance to get into the group, even after the graffiti episode, was she ready for their black handshake? She was a decision away from knowing who these THC members were. And perhaps then to knowing about Anara's truth. Five minutes of intense mental-wrestle later she messaged Tavish: *Will you be okay if I woo Ahaan? It would be fake but I need to know how you'll feel?* She sent it. It was read almost immediately, but there was no response. Should she take that as a 'no'? Suddenly the phone rang and Tavish's name popped up. Kisha dreaded to take the call. Something told her it would decide both their journeys.

FOURTEEN

KISHA HEARD TAVISH OUT WITH THE UTMOST PATIENCE. He was speaking very fast and seemed extremely excited. He told her that he had figured out a way and that she wouldn't have to involve Ahaan after all. Namashi, he had discovered, was in Lucknow. They could go, meet him and come back in a day. She understood Tavish really did not want her wooing Ahaan. If she had to do it, he wanted it to be their last resort. So did she, if she was being honest. It was no joke to make someone fall in love with you just like that. And what about the consequences? Who would be responsible for it? Kisha agreed to Tavish's plan, hoping it would spare involving more people and getting caught up in a deeper mess.

Flying to Lucknow was even more of an adventure than visiting Rajveer's place in Gurugram. Kisha and Tavish followed the same modus operandi as they had done for the visit to Rajveer's home. Tavish booked the tickets, the cost of which they split between them. The money for the trip was smartly managed within the monthly budget they got from their respective parents. And a couple of discreet arrangements later they were ready to go.

On the journey, Kisha noticed the little things Tavish did for her. Since she was not too familiar with Indian airports, Tavish led the way. He took care of all the travel arrangements and made sure she was carrying her ID. She was touched to see how he cared for her. He didn't let her stand in the boarding pass queue at the kiosk. They didn't have luggage so he simply asked her to sit so he could wait in the queue. When his turn came he punched their PNR on the kiosk machine and collected their boarding passes. Kisha's eyes were all the time on him. The way he was making her feel protective was giving her gooseflesh every now and then. After they were done with their security check and were waiting for boarding to begin, he got her coffee and cookies, anticipating her hunger. *How is he reading me so smoothly? Is that normal?* Kisha was enjoying every second of it. They sat together, beside their boarding gate, munching on the cookies. Tavish was talking continuously—from his latest music fad to his favourite travel destination to his childhood—but Kisha was far away. She was lost in his words, in his scent, in him. She revelled in his presence. When they boarded the flight, she saw that their seats were at the end of the aircraft and there was no one else seated in that row. A secret thrill ran up Kisha's spine.

As the flight took off, it was like her heart too had taken off. She was sitting by the window, while Tavish sat beside her. After only a few minutes, he dozed off, his mouth open like a baby's. Kisha kept looking at him, unable to look away from his perfectly chiselled jaw. Drawn to his perfectly angular face, Kisha moved close and brought her mouth close to his, feeling his breath on her. She blushed and stopped herself, giggling awkwardly. It was then that she concluded that perhaps the one thing she felt would never happen to her, had finally come to be. She was in love with Tavish Mathur. Kisha kept smiling to herself till there was an announcement that the flight was about to land.

The two took a cab to Namashi's place to Jopling Road, in Lucknow, hoping to find him there. Unlike the previous time, when Tavish had reached out to Rajveer, he hadn't been able to call earlier and fix an appointment. He didn't know any common friend or senior who could connect him to Namashi. Kisha understood he was taking a shot in the dark only for her and her quest to know Anara's truth.

As it happened, Namashi was home but the meeting turned out to be neither fruitful nor a waste. Just like Rajveer, Namashi, too, didn't have a problem talking to them about his time in Fairmont High. He spoke slowly and seemed to lose track of his thoughts often, which frustrated Kisha, but she said nothing. He told them that life had changed for him from the time he dropped out of Fairmont High. On being asked about what had happened to him there, he told them his story.

Namashi fell in love with a girl by the name of Shobhita. It was all hunky-dory in the beginning but he got the shock of his life when one day she complained about him, saying he was abusing her. She presented their personal chats as proof. The same intimate chat, which Namashi had exchanged with her when they were in love, suddenly read completely different, in the context of abuse. Namashi was destroyed. He didn't know why Shobhita did it, why she took a complete U-turn on their love story or why she levied false allegations on him.

It didn't matter, for Namashi never did get any answers. She stopped replying to his texts and his calls went unanswered. His parents begged her to withdraw the case but she did not relent. Finally, unable to bear the humiliation and hate that came his way, Namashi decided to leave school. The incident affected him so deeply that he dropped out that year, came to his home town and just spent a year at home, recovering from the setback. He joined the local school the year after, but he was never the same. Listening to Namashi, Tavish and Kisha looked at each other. Even if Namashi didn't know it, they understood why Shobhita may have done it. The Heartbreak Club. They would have to talk to her. It also meant, Kisha figured, that Shobhita had passed her black handshake and must have been part of the Heartbreak Club till she passed out.

'Where's Shobhita now?' Kisha asked. She knew if they could reach her then a lot of their questions could be answered. She was, in all probability, an ex-member.

'Who knows. Last I heard, she was in the US,' Namashi said nonchalantly.

Tavish and Kisha were crestfallen. Flying to Lucknow was one thing but the US? They wouldn't be able to reach Shobhita. They could connect to her via social media but the chances of her ignoring them were high. She was an offender and wouldn't want to talk openly.

'I think Shobhita was tested by THC. She passed,' Tavish said as they boarded their flight back to Delhi.

'Exactly what I was thinking. So, at least we now know one person who could have been in the Heartbreak Club until a year back.'

'If only this had happened last year, we could have reached Shobhita. She was in school at that time,' Tavish said in a frustrated tone.

'But we were destined to meet this year I guess. It's okay,' Kisha said. Tavish gave her a warm, acknowledging smile.

'It also tells us that the members indeed keep changing. They must have included someone else when Shobhita passed out.'

'Most importantly, I think the question should be where does Anara fit into all this,' Tavish said. He was bang on, Kisha thought. Though she had more information now than she did earlier, Kisha was still clueless about what happened to Anara. Did someone break her heart so badly that she got too depressed to want to remain in society? Was she with THC? But as a perpetrator or a victim? Kisha kept thinking and finally the answer was clear to her. Her sister had to be a victim of the club's nefarious ways. If she had been the perpetrator then she would have been in school and someone else would have disappeared in her place.

It had been a long day and, on the flight, Kisha felt sleepy. She put her head on Tavish's shoulder and closed her eyes. When he touched her face lightly, Kisha neither moved nor said anything. All through, she kept wondering if he, too, was as attracted to her as she was to him. Why else would he touch her? She didn't want to open her eyes and realise it was a dream. So, Kisha kept her eyes closed, while leaning on his shoulder even more. She could smell the cologne he was wearing and it filled her senses. From now on whenever she would inhale this scent, it would remind her of Tavish. The fragrance had a face now. What tickled her was the way their fingers were grazing each other's constantly.

When a slight turbulence occurred mid-sky, their fingers intertwined, as if instinctively. The symbolism of it—that they would be together during life's turbulence—struck Kisha and she blushed with her eyes closed. She heard the landing announcement by the pilot and was immediately sad. The next moment she felt a tap on her arm. It was Tavish. She pretended to wake up with a start.

'I'm so sorry,' she said, while in her mind she was ruing the fact that they had to land. Why couldn't they be in the sky forever? Tavish smiled at her as if he had heard her thoughts. They landed soon after and reached Fairmont High before night. They discussed what their next step should be during their cab ride till school.

'Do we have a choice?' Tavish said. Kisha knew what he was actually asking. He wanted to know if there was a chance that she would let go of her pursuit. Kisha took her time and then said, 'I really need to know what happened to Anara di. That was my main reason for coming here.'

'Then we both know what you have to do.'

Pass the test, Kisha completed in her mind.

The whole thing—to make someone fall in love with you only to break the person's heart—was weird for Kisha. Why would a set of people think that way? Is that what had happened to her sister? If so, then what could have made THC choose Anara? Going by what she'd heard from Rajveer and Namashi, there was a strong possibility that either Anara was asked, like Shobhita, to pass the test or she was chosen, like Rajveer, to be a part of the club, but she turned them down. As a result, whatever it was that she desired with all her heart was snatched from her. Or, the other possibility was, someone broke Anara's heart and she was so damaged that she had to vanish. Then there was Selena's claim that Anara was bi. A tired Kisha realised her head was aching and she couldn't take more for the day as she turned in for the night.

The next morning, when Kisha went to her class, she noticed Ahaan sitting my himself. Just a few weeks ago, she had rebuffed his attentions and now she had to woo him. It was not only awkward but also ridiculous. How would she convince Ahaan when she felt so fake about it that it made her sick. Yet, it had to be done.

She started glancing at Ahaan in an obvious way, during the class. She was sure he'd notice her long stares from the corner of his eye, and he did! After the class, Kisha prayed that Ahaan would come up to her. And that's what happened.

'Hi Kisha, did you want to tell me something? I think I saw you looking at me a few times,' he asked uncertainly.

It worked, Kisha thought and said aloud, 'I am having some trouble with the Maths lessons. I know you're good at it, so I was thinking maybe we could study together in the library? It would help me understand certain concepts better.' Kisha hoped a combination of helplessness and flattery would help win Ahaan over.

'Yeah, sure. Why not!' The glimmer in Ahaan's eyes told her that her method was spot on.

They went to the library where they whispered and laughed together, rather than study. Ahaan's excitement was palpable. He kept explaining some formulae or the other, along with discussing random things with the girl who he was smitten with. Once done, he asked if he could walk with her till the girls' hostel. Kisha agreed.

'Today is easily my happiest day,' Ahaan said with a broad smile.

'Why?'

'The girl I'm crazy about just spent so much time with me!'

Wow, he is NOT subtle at all, Kisha thought and forced a smile. Ahaan suddenly hugged her and then said, 'Good night.' Kisha too headed inside the girls' hostel.

Ahaan walked away a happy soul. But he wasn't the only one who was happy. From the second-floor window of the girls' hostel, Vega smiled as she sat recording a video of them from her room. Finally, she would get a chance to erase Kisha from Tavish's life. Vega sent the video of Ahaan hugging Kisha to Tavish with a message: *Are you two in an open relationship? Interesting.*

FIFTEEN

Tavish didn't respond to Vega, but he did message Kisha: *Meet me RIGHT NOW in the field.*

The caps conveyed an urgency and so Kisha skipped her meal and made a dash for the field. Vega noticed it and smirked. She was pretty sure who Kisha was running to, leaving her meal. Tavish may have chosen silence as his reply to her message but she knew it had triggered this reaction. The usually bland canteen food, which Vega always complained about, suddenly tasted good to her.

―

Kisha saw Tavish was already standing at the corner of the rugby field. As she walked up to him, she knew he must be aware of her presence but he didn't budge. Was he angry? She went up to him and said, 'Tavish, all okay?'

He turned to face her. Something in his eyes told her he was in pain.

'Kish, I think we should have some rules for this fake wooing of yours.'

Kisha frowned wondering where this was coming from. A flurry of images flashed through her mind and it stopped at the point when Ahaan had hugged her outside the girls' hostel. *Had Tavish seen them? Did that upset him?*

'Is it the hug?' she asked him, pointblank.

'It doesn't matter what it is, but there should be rules.'

By now Kisha had understood one thing about Tavish—while he was confrontational, he was also passive aggressive. He would express his displeasure but never too directly. He would only give a hint of it, and then, when you would pester him for the reason, he would say it didn't matter. As if he wanted you to peep into his mind to know what he thought, without him verbalising directly. It was frustrating, but that's how it was.

'So, it is the hug. You were there?'

'Vega sent me a picture.'

Kisha sighed in exasperation. Vega would have to be dealt with, she made a mental note.

'Tavish, he hugged me and it was sudden, but I'm cool with rules.'

'Good. I propose no physical contact, no sharing of intimate pictures and no "I love you,"' Tavish said. It sounded like he had rehearsed the rules numerous times before telling her. Kisha smiled. She could have pulled his cheeks at the moment. She decided to tease him a bit.

'I understand the first two but the third? I'm trying to woo him and I would have to—'

'You can't love two people at the same time.'

'Is that a rule too?' Kisha was having a ball toying with Tavish in this way. The fact that he was affected by her teasing, emboldened her further.

'That's a given. Like it's a given you can't breathe and die at the same time,' he said.

'That means you are saying I should reserve the "I love you" part for someone else?' she said with a twinkle in her eye.

It was then that Tavish understood that she was teasing. He upped the ante.

'I think you've been claimed by someone already, don't you?'

Though the statement wasn't as emotionally sensitive as Kisha, a woke soul, would have liked, but the way he said the word *claimed*, made her go weak in the knees. In that very moment the word made her feel like the most desirable girl on the planet. She didn't know what happened to her as, driven by an impulse, Kisha took two steps to come closer to him. Before Tavish could realise what was happening, Kisha leaned her head forward intending to kiss his cheeks. Tavish moved his face at the last minute and their lips met. She closed her eyes instantly. Then let him go.

'I dare you to break my trust in you, Tavish. And I dare myself to break your trust in me. I would rather die.'

Tavish had never seen her so intense. He didn't say anything. The way she sounded, he knew she meant every word of it. They hugged. The quietude around made their heartbeats audible to the other. Both their hearts were racing as if trying to catch up with each other. Then they started beating in rhythm, attaining normalcy, as Kisha and Tavish looked deep into each other's eyes.

'Thanks,' Tavish said. Kisha hugged him tight again. *He* was *hers*.

Kisha continued to pursue Ahaan, keeping in mind the three rules which Tavish had laid down. Not that she needed to have worried. Ahaan was always ready for Kisha and she had to do little else than just give him some attention. Every time they met, Ahaan gave her a reversible sketch which Kisha expressed heartfelt gratitude for. But Kisha also knew she had to maintain a balance. She couldn't get too close, too soon. Every connection had levels. She wanted to first start with friendship and then let things develop slowly. One day, on their way to the library, Ahaan and she got talking about their past.

'Well, I don't really miss my life in the UK too much. My parents are no longer together. It's good to get away from all that for a bit,' Kisha said.

'Did that tick your sister off?' Ahaan asked.

'No,' Kisha said. She realised she had never thought about it from that perspective. But why would Anara put her life at risk for her parents? And why would she stop communicating with Kisha, if that was the case?

'I mean ... not that I know of,' she said, correcting herself.

'I always feel we are all full of secrets. And we crave for that one person who could become our secret-keeper,' Ahaan said shyly.

'What secrets do you have?' Kisha steered the conversation, so Ahaan could talk more than she did. She noticed him looking around. There were students milling about, but nobody was sitting close to them.

'I've grown up with violent parents,' he said. The seriousness of his expression hit Kisha.

'I'm so sorry, Ahaan. Did they beat you up?'

'No. They used to beat each other up. And they continue to do so. That's one reason they put me into this school. My grandparents insisted on it since they thought it would have a bad influence on me.'

'Of course. They were right.'

'Yeah. But they were too late.'

Kisha frowned and asked, 'What do you mean?'

Ahaan gave out a short mirthless laugh. 'Would you believe it if I say,' he paused and looked around, and added in a whisper, 'that I still wet my bed.' He shrugged sadly.

Kisha was taken aback by his admission but checked her expression. Anyway Ahaan looked visibly embarrassed. He'd not only confessed something which no one would admit publicly, but he had also said it to a girl he liked. He must have squashed his male ego in order to come out with that confession. Did she make him that comfortable that he told her such a deep secret of his?

By the time Kisha returned to her dorm that evening, she had started seeing Ahaan in a different light. She felt sympathy for him. She understood that he didn't need a girlfriend, what he needed was a best friend. Maybe it was his naivete, but no boy would share such a secret with his girl. For that, one needed a close friend, a confidante. A girlfriend or boyfriend may not be one's best friend, but she wondered if Ahaan even knew the difference. In all honesty, she felt bad for him.

Weirdly enough, since that day, Kisha started feeling a little protective about Ahaan. She started taking certain decisions for him, and was always full of suggestions for him, whether he needed them or not. She was borderline patronising Ahaan, thinking she was helping someone in need of emotional help. Ahaan didn't complain or show any sign of resentment, which made her continue her behaviour. Though she didn't tell Tavish about Ahaan's bed-wetting, she used to update him on a daily basis on what she was up to with him. Kisha realised she would have to speed up the process of fake wooing him, leading to breaking his heart. The Heartbreak Club hadn't given her a timeline, but she knew the exchange program was for six months and she was already in the third month. She decided to discuss it with Tavish.

'So, I was thinking, should we talk about how I can take this to the next level?' She thought it was best if the suggestion came from Tavish. If he was involved, knew her plan of action the chances of misunderstandings between them were minimum.

'What do you mean?'

'I don't have much time, Tavish. I know Ahaan is comfortable with me. We have to think of the next steps now.' She noticed a sharp glance from Tavish. He didn't say anything. Since Kisha had begun wooing Ahaan, she and Tavish weren't meeting during the day at all. They always had to sneak out of their hostel rooms and meet somewhere in the campus after dark. During day he was her captain. That's all. And it wasn't as if Tavish and she had had a long relationship after realising their feelings for each other. That too had just begun to develop when this whole fake-wooing-of-Ahaan plan had unfolded. They wanted to spend time together but that was proving impossible.

'Have you realised something, Kisha?' Tavish asked.

'What?'

'Since the last ten days, every time we meet, we only talk about Ahaan. We barely talk about ourselves.'

Kisha wished she could counter that, but Tavish was right. It was a fact. It was as if Tavish and she had gotten into a relationship only to discuss Ahaan.

'I know and it frustrates me too. But once I break his heart, this will all stop. That's why I want to get to the next step without delay.' Kisha tried to find hope in the entire mess they were in.

'And who knows, by that time you may have to go back to London,' Tavish said bitterly.

Kisha felt like crying. Tavish was right, a little too right, in fact. There were moments when it was better to not state the truth, even if the truth was staring one in the face. This was one of those moments. On the one hand she had to find out what had happened to Anara. That was the whole reason for her to come all the way to India. But on the other hand, her first love story was getting extinguished even before it had blossomed fully.

Kisha wanted to say a lot but had no words. Tavish had a lot of words but didn't want to say much, lest they became the reason for a break in their nascent relationship. His silence told her he wouldn't be suggesting anything as far as Ahaan was concerned. She understood this was coming from a place of hurt. And from Tavish's point of view, the hurt was justified. Kisha left with a resolve to decide and act quickly. The only way she could heal Tavish's hurt was to break Ahaan's heart. Sooner than later. Or else, she would have to simply give up chasing THC, seeking Anara's truth and enjoy the romance that life had thrown her way in the form of Tavish Mathur.

When Kisha came back to the hostel, Jas came to her room with some food.

'I saw you dash from the meal room. All okay?' Jas asked. Kisha felt so overwhelmed that all she could do was hold her and cry. She was having a full-blown meltdown and needed someone to support her.

'Hey, what happened?' Jas was visibly surprised.

Kisha knew she couldn't discuss her situation with anybody. One little nugget of information was all it would take to lead to another, and soon her entire attempt to reach the club may stand negated.

'Nothing. It's just one of those nights,' Kisha said wiping her tears. Jas wasn't convinced but she knew Kisha enough by then, that if she had decided not to share something she wouldn't.

The next morning, while Kisha was in the swimming pool, getting in her swim practice, she noticed Tavish come there and dive in. He swam right up to where she was. He removed his goggles. She removed hers. Next, she felt his hand on hers.

'I love you.'

The moment he uttered those words, time stopped for Kisha. And she thought her breath had stopped too. But she heard him continue, 'Let's get this done quickly and get the focus back on us. I kept thinking about it last night. I don't want to lose you, Kish,' Tavish said passionately.

Only Kisha knew how disturbed her sleep was, a night before, but suddenly after hearing Tavish's words, she felt fresh within. As Kisha kept looking deep into his eyes, she felt his hand go below the water. His fingers touched her belly, and with light strokes of his fingertips, he traced the letter 'T' on it. Kisha didn't know what to focus on. The new found hope his words gave her or the deeply sexual urge his touch connected her to.

SIXTEEN

AHAAN WAS SURPRISED WHEN VEGA APPROACHED HIM IN the school café. He was having a migraine attack and had thought gulping some black coffee would help. Out of nowhere, Vega had appeared by his side.

'Hey Ahaan, how have you been?'

'I'm good, Vega. You?'

'Never been better. Listen, I wanted to know something.'

'Tell me,' he said taking a sip from his black coffee. He wished she wasn't bothering him right now, in the middle of his migraine.

'Are you and Kisha a couple?'

Ahaan wasn't expecting this. He found himself shaking his head at Vega in disagreement.

'Oh, I thought otherwise,' Vega said.

'Really? What made you think so?'

Vega looked around as if she was about to blast a truth bomb on Ahaan, and nobody else should hear it explode. She said, 'Kisha was telling me that she badly wants to kiss you, as she finds you irresistibly cute.'

Ahaan couldn't suppress his shock. Though he couldn't help but feel pleased as well.

'She said that?'

'How else do you think I guessed you two are having a

scene? Though now I know my guess is wrong. Anyway, she is such a darling. Has helped me so much in academics.'

'That she is. We solve our Maths problems together.'

Vega saw Ahaan blush and knew her plan would work out with ease.

'Ahaan, I'm here with a seemingly odd request, but I'm doing it because she has been such a good friend to me. See, Kisha is very nice and sweet. And she likes you a lot, but she'll never directly ask you to kiss her. I wanted to request you if you could,' she paused and noticed Ahaan's attention on her intensify further, then said, 'kiss her I mean.'

Ahaan looked a bit sceptical. 'I don't know if that's the best idea, Vega,' he said.

'What? Why? It's not a request I'm making to satisfy some fantasy of mine,' Vega said and noticed incredulity on Ahaan's face.

'You don't believe me?' Vega opened her phone to a WhatsApp chat. She showed it to Ahaan. He read it with utmost curiosity, which slowly changed to excitement by the time he reached the end of the chat. The chat was between Kisha and Vega and she had explicitly mentioned that she had fallen for Ahaan and wanted to seal it with a kiss. The only problem was that she was scared to take the first step.

'Now do you believe me?' Vega said, noticing a smile on Ahaan's face.

'She won't mind if I kiss her?'

'You've read the chat. What do you think?'

Ahaan smiled and shook his head.

'Go for it, dude. I would say, the sooner you do it the better. How about today, when you guys go to the library? Maybe she'll actually end up proposing to you after the kiss. Our entire batch would love to know you guys are dating.' Vega put on her best smile. She was hugely relieved this was going a whole lot easier than she had expected.

By the time Ahaan walked out of the café, he was determined to give Kisha what he had been made to believe she was craving for. Little did he know that Vega had changed her friend's name to Kisha, had that fake chat and shown it to him. If he had checked the phone number, he would have known he was being cheated, but he, too, desperately wanted the lie to be true. He had checked Kisha's WhatsApp DP on Vega's phone, and had found it to be the same as the one that appeared on his phone. That's all it had taken to convince him.

Now that she set the plan in motion, Vega kept an eye on Ahaan. She intentionally stayed away from Kisha, lest she become suspicious and see through her, but she kept trailing Ahaan. Soon, she knew her moment had arrived. In between two classes, there was a free period. Vega saw Kisha and Ahaan leave the classroom together. They usually spent their free periods in the library, so she followed them there. Sure enough, they went to the library. Vega sat at some distance from them but at an angle where she could secretly record them without being obvious about it. She couldn't figure out what they were talking about, but she kept the video recording of her phone on. Seeing Ahaan's jittery body language, she knew the kiss would happen any time now. And it did! It was sudden, it was abrupt but it had happened. And it had been captured. Vega was overjoyed.

For someone seeing the video without context, it would seem like Kisha too participated in the kiss. The reality was she was taken aback when Ahaan had kissed her and had pushed him back in two seconds. She had not only pushed him, but slapped him as well. And then, before Ahaan knew what was happening, she walked out of the library looking pissed off. And violated.

But those few seconds were enough for Vega to get what she wanted. She sat there looking at a confused Ahaan run out behind Kisha. Vega then calmly worked on the video, editing out the push, the slap and the initial time when they'd been talking. The three second video was the final draft, which she sent to Tavish, hoping that Kisha would forever be gone from his life. She couldn't help but chuckle to herself before sauntering out of the library, softly whistling her favourite Rihanna song.

Kisha's whole body was warm. It had been a while since she had been triggered in this way. And she knew if she wasn't alone, she would end up doing something which may push her to rehab again. She didn't attend the next class and went straight to her hostel room.

Ahaan, realising something had gone wrong, ran behind her after just a few seconds. Not finding Kisha in the class, he turned to Vega afterwards.

'I kissed Kisha but she ended up slapping me. But you said she had told you she wanted it. What's going on?' Ahaan whined.

Vega looked at him and smiled. 'Really, lover boy? What can I do if she slapped you?'

'But-but...you were the—'

'Fuck off or else I will slap you ten more times,' said Vega, raising her pitch.

She didn't stop for his reaction and walked off. Ahaan found her sudden change in tone confusing. Had he made a mistake? He was in two minds whether to call Kisha or not. Then he decided to do it. It rang once before being disconnected. He tried again only to hear that the phone was switched off. Ahaan knew instantly he didn't make a mistake. It was a blunder.

When Kisha entered her hostel room, she saw someone had left a small soft toy for her by the door. It was a panda, her favourite animal. It couldn't be Ahaan, could it? Maybe he knew he might be slapped and had planned an apology in advance? She picked it up, simmering with anger, and went inside. The entire kissing episode distressed her. She felt violated, but she was also worried about Tavish and his rules. Would she be able to tell him about this? Would he understand that she had zero consent in this? She saw Ahaan was calling her but she didn't want to talk to him. When he tried the second time, she switched the phone off for a good half an hour, after which she switched it back on. Then, taking a deep breath, she was about to call Tavish when her phone rang, flashing his name.

'I was just about to call you. Something—'

'How was the kiss?' Tavish cut in. 'I thought we had laid out some ground rules.' Tavish not only sounded mean but disgusted and deeply hurt. Kisha simply couldn't take his tone.

'Who told you?' she asked, wondering if he was there in the library when the incident had happened. If he'd seen it with his own eyes, he surely would know she had been caught off guard by Ahaan. But it was clear from the tone of his voice, he didn't have firsthand knowledge of the matter. Someone must have conveyed it to him.

'Nice to know that your concern is who told me, rather than what you did.'

'Tavish, please. Don't react before I clarify things.'

'There's nothing to clarify. I thought we were in love. Clearly, you want to experiment. But I don't. So, just buzz off.' He ended the call. Never before had anyone cut the call while she still had so much to say. Kisha didn't know what hurt her more, Ahaan's unabashed presumptuousness or Tavish's naked ire. She understood that Tavish was angry, but didn't he trust her? Shouldn't he give her a chance to explain, if he loved her? She cried her heart out for a while, but then, washed her face and got up. Her face set in a firm resolve, she walked out of the hostel. On her way, she called Ahaan, who sounded relieved when he answered her call. Before he could say much, she just asked him where he was exactly. When he mumbled that he was in his room, she asked him to meet her at the school café and disconnected the call.

When Kisha entered the café, Ahaan was already there, waiting for her eagerly. She approached him like a lioness on a hunt.

'We'll talk about what you did later. Right now, I want to know how Tavish found out about what happened in the library?'

'Huh? I don't know what you are talking about.'

'Don't play innocent with me, Ahaan. You come clean to me now or I'm going to the principal and lodging a complaint against you. What you did was reprehensible,' Kisha said assuming he was the one who had told Tavish about the kiss.

'Look, Kisha, I am sorry. I only did what Vega told me to do. I thought you wanted me to. And I have no idea about Tavish. You have to believe me!'

Kisha frowned. In the few days she had spent with Ahaan, she had not got the impression that he would lie. She asked him to explain and Ahaan blurted out the entire conversation he had had with Vega that morning. He even mentioned the chat. Kisha's jaws were clenched by the time Ahaan finished.

'I'm really sorry, Kisha. I didn't know—'

'It's alright,' Kisha said, realising Ahaan had been manipulated, just like Tavish. She took a few deep breaths and controlled her raging urge to break Vega's head. She left the café without another word.

Kisha knew confronting Vega in the hostel would alert the warden. She went to her room, after meeting Ahaan to calm herself down. She tried to remember the tips she had learnt in rehab. The next day, she waited for Vega outside the academic block. When she saw Vega arrive with her groupies after her classes, Kisha went to her and, looking dart straight into her eyes, said, 'We need to talk.'

Vega lifted her chin in defiance. 'Let's do it here.'

'Why do you have to play the bitch in my life? I, till now, haven't done anything to you and yet you are out to make my life difficult.'

'Because you are being a bitch to me by being in Tavish's life,' Vega retorted. It seemed like she was ready for the confrontation.

'*He* chose me over you. So, if you have to complain, do it to him. Why are you assassinating my character?'

'How I choose to deal with it is my wish,' Vega said defiantly.

'Then I'll choose to break your head. I've had some experience in that area, trust me.'

Jas came running. She held Kisha by the shoulder and pulled her away in the nick of time.

'Tell her to stay away from my business. Or else I wouldn't mind a second trip to rehab,' Kisha shouted before being dragged away by Jas. Vega, too, walked off with her groupies.

'What are you doing? If any teacher had seen you fighting, both of you would've been suspended,' Jas said. Kisha stood with her hands on her waist, not at all pleased that Jas had pulled her away before she could punch Vega. She marched right towards a nearby wall and punched it, in angst, injuring her wrist in the process. Jas took her to the hostel room, brought her some water and calmed her down. It took an hour, but Kisha began to breath normally again, though her mind was still in a state of chaos.

She called Tavish, later in the night, but his phone was switched off. It was too late to go to the boys' hostel, besides she wasn't sure Tavish would even meet her. She sent him messages but could see that they didn't get delivered. She just needed one chance to explain herself. She understood how angry and upset he must've been on seeing the video. She would've been upset too, if a video of Tavish kissing another girl reached her. But she deserved an opportunity to explain herself. Not everything was what it looked like. He would have to understand.

'Jas, do you know any guy in the boys' hostel who can inform Tavish that I want to talk to him urgently?' Kisha asked. Jas immediately called Surya, Tavish's close buddy.

'Hey Jas, what's up?' Surya said, picking her call on the second ring.

'All cool. Listen up, is Tavish nearby?'

'He was. He just went to his room. What happened?'

'Can you please ask him to call Kisha or take her call? It's super urgent.'

'Umm, okay. Doing it.'

Surya ended the call. Kisha sat waiting with bated breath, staring at her phone's screen, expecting it to flash Tavish's name any moment. Instead it was Jas phone that flashed with Surya's name, instead.

'Did you ask him?' Jas said picking up the call.

'Tavish doesn't want to talk to Kisha,' Surya said.

After a brief pause, Jas said, 'Okay.'

When Jas relayed to Kisha what Surya had told her, she felt like she had been stabbed. What hurt her was that Tavish's avoidance meant that he had already assumed that she was the culprit. He'd judged her without hearing her side of the story. After Jas left the room, Kisha cried her eyes out. It was well past midnight when, lying motionless like a corpse, she heard her phone vibrating. She picked it up and saw that it was Tavish calling. She let the phone vibrate. *Could she imagine a love story with a guy, who would listen to others and form an opinion about her and not even give her a chance to say her piece?* Kisha wondered, as her eyes moistened with warm tears. Though the phone stopped vibrating after some time but her tears didn't stop.

SEVENTEEN

KISHA WOKE UP WITH A START. SHE GRASPED HER PHONE and was relieved to see it was early enough for her to get ready in time for her classes. There was no message from Tavish, only the call she had willfully missed. There was a notification on the school app. A message from Bishop. Her heart skipped a beat. She read it immediately.

There's something by your door.

Kisha jumped out of her bed and dashed to the main door of her room. Right outside lay a soft toy, another Panda, but with a note this time. Letters had been cut and pasted from magazines to form the message of the note. The message made Kisha frown. It read:

Hello, crush.

What did that mean? Was the Bishop of THC trying to tell her he had a crush on her? The next second she had another thought. Perhaps this is a trick. She picked up the panda and kept it beside the one she had found a day back.

When Kisha went to her class, she found Ahaan sitting alone with a hangdog expression. He had been messaging her constantly, apologising nonstop. Kisha ignored him and took her seat but her mind was in a mess. Here was a boy who was sorry for what he had done, knowing well he wasn't directly responsible. Afterall, he had been misled into believing a falsehood. And then there was Tavish who claimed to love her and yet wasn't even ready to hear her out. What was he thinking when he called her late last night? He would talk to her whenever he felt up to it? Why hadn't he picked up her calls when she was trying desperately to talk to him? As the teacher droned on about the binomial theorem in class, Kisha turned to face Ahaan. 'It's okay,' she mouthed to his incredulous face. Ahaan smiled at her, mouthing a silent 'Thank you' and clasping his hands in relief.

After the class, Kisha was running down the stairs to the lab for her practical, when suddenly Tavish appeared in front of her.

'You do know, that not answering your captain's phone call can land you in a lot of trouble?'

Kisha's face was impassive. She simply looked at Tavish and said, 'Please go ahead and register a complaint against me, captain. I'm ready to face the consequences.' She tried to sidestep him and move ahead, but Tavish stopped her.

'I'm curious as to what makes you so haughty even after getting caught doing whatever you were up to with Ahaan.'

'It's called the truth, Tavish. And sometimes even the truth can have different versions. Do try to understand that when you can,' Kisha said and pushed her way ahead of him.

'It's clear you guys were kissing. What fucking truth are you talking about?' Tavish called after her.

Kisha stopped, turned around, and said in a spiteful tone, 'I think it's best I leave before you say more things that make me lose all respect for you.'

With those words, she stormed off. If he really wanted to talk to her and know the truth, he would have to discard the arrogance and judgmental attitude. Kisha was dead sure about that.

Kisha took her seat in the lab, though her mind was still far away. She realised what exactly had ticked her off about Tavish when he stopped her. A part of it was what had bothered her the night before—he had proclaimed her guilty without bothering to listen to her side of things. But another part of it was also how much he reminded her of her father, Prithibi. Her father had the same arrogance and self-righteous attitude towards Ranya, for reasons Kisha could never fathom. It irked and angered her. Her mother wasn't perfect but she would try to have conversations and sort out their problems, only to be met by Prithibi's barbs. To Kisha it seemed as if her mother never got the respect she deserved in the house. And she knew even Anara felt the same.

Her parents had had a love marriage. Or so she and her sister were told. From the time Kisha was old enough to remember, she could never find a trace of love in their marriage. There may not have been screaming and shouting in the house, but there was always an air of suppressed anger, a brewing frustration and a palpable negativity. Kisha could see her mom put in the effort even as her father failed to acknowledge it. It was as if Prithibi had taken an oath that he would never be impressed with Ranya, no matter how much she tried. Kisha, in fact, had once overheard a conversation between Ranya and Anara. Her elder sister, too, had the same question for their mother.

'Mom, what exactly is wrong with dad?'

Ranya was dusting the room but when she spoke, her voice quivered with emotion.

'He is a *man*. That's what's wrong with him.'

'What do you mean?' Anara had asked.

'It's rare to find a man who stays interested and attentive towards his partner even after his sexual and domestic conquest is over. If they were truthful, married men would confess that they no longer found their partners to be engaging. That's how they are hardwired—once the chase is over, the dullness of domesticity bores them. And that's exactly what is wrong with your dad. He isn't interested. Shame that "not being interested" is not a criminal offense, only a moral and emotional one. And it doesn't matter what others say, everything from sagging skin to a fading figure, to the quality of sex has a role to play in it.'

There was a silence that followed Ranya's monologue. And after that, all Kisha heard was their mother's sniffles as she continued to dust the room.

Kisha wasn't sure about her sister, but for her that had been a watershed moment. Her mother's words, and the thoughts propelling those words, stayed with her. And now when she remembered that scene, she wondered if her mother had been right: all men were just the same. Perhaps women were pursuing the wrong things in love. It wasn't important whom you loved the most, what was important was to find someone whose love would undergo a delayed erosion. Because, if her mother was to be believed, every man's love eroded over time. And just when she thought she had met someone who made her believe in love, someone she thought would defy the theory her mother had laid down, life had delivered a cruel dose of reality.

Kisha thought about Ranya and how maybe she, too, had been unfair to her mother. The moment her class ended, she called her. Ranya answered and sounded genuinely happy to hear from her. Kisha asked her about what had been happening, enquired about Fluff, and asked if she would want to know what had happened to Anara.

'What do you mean *if* I would want to? I damn sure want to know. Your father and I spoke about this many times. But I don't know why he is so detached from the entire matter. And here I'm caught up with so many things. Need to sort them out before I can plan ahead.'

'I get it.'

Kisha felt proud of her mother. Truth be told, she had never thought highly of Ranya before because she had never seen her mother take any bold decision in life. She was more like the one who always cried over split milk. But recent conversations had made her look at Ranya with a completely renewed perspective. She sounded like a woman who was preparing to take charge of her own life.

The next few days went by without anything eventful happening. Kisha kept to herself, avoiding meeting or even talking about Tavish. Ahaan and she continued spending time together. She knew this was the only way she had to find out more about her elder sister. She just didn't know how she would break Ahaan's heart. Kisha felt torn and unsettled. She felt she was living a lie. She didn't love Ahaan, but had to project that she did. The two were always together, be it in class, the library, the swimming pool, even meeting for late night chats. She knew Ahaan was in love with her, even though he hadn't professed it in words. Maybe, Kisha thought, he was scared after the slap incident.

She couldn't be more into the whole fake-wooing bit than she already was because of one simple fact: she didn't actually love him. She still loved Tavish. Her attraction towards him was still strong and sometimes her heart ached when she saw him on campus. There were times when Kisha thought she spotted him looking at her longingly. She wasn't talking to him, but wondered whether he too was yearning for her. It had become a fight of egos, she knew.

One night, Jas brought some beers to the girl's hostel and she and Kisha decided to get drunk in her room. By the time she was a bottle down, Kisha was blabbering about herself and referring to Tavish's behavior as a red flag.

'He could have given me a chance. What chance! He should have heard me out. Doesn't he love me? Who was it who kissed me in the rugby field then? His twin?'

Jas' eyes widened on hearing about their kiss.

'Did you guys fuck there?'

'No! We kissed. A peck. It was almost chaste. And I believed in it, Jas. I believed in him. You tell me what I should do. I don't like Ahaan but he does what I want Tavish to do.'

'Pursue you?'

'No! He hears me out. Ahaan always hears me out. Tavish doesn't. Our love story had only started damnit,' she slurred with moistened eyes.

Seeing Kisha's tears, Jas' heart sank. The effect of the beer washed right off.

'I'm amazed that a guy like Tavish, knowing the kiss was not your fault, is still so harsh on you,' Jas said. Kisha had told her about the kiss with Ahaan and of Vega's involvement.

'He doesn't know it wasn't my fault. That's the whole goddamn point.'

Jas couldn't believe her ears. In the next two minutes she made sure Kisha coughed up what had gone wrong between Tavish and her. Once Kisha fell asleep, Jas called Tavish.

It was raining the next day. Kisha had forgotten what all she had blabbered to Jas the night before. All she knew was that she felt stifled. As if something was pent up within her. Ahaan asked if they could go to the library.

'Sure, let's go,' she said. On their way to the library, they ran into Tavish, who looked at Ahaan in a condescending manner, and then, glancing at Kisha, said, 'We need to talk.'

Something in his eyes—genuineness and maybe some remorse— stopped her from saying a blatant no. Instead, she found herself turn towards Ahaan and say, 'Will you excuse me? I'll call you.' Ahaan nodded, like an obedient boy, and left.

Kisha followed Tavish out. She had an umbrella but he was getting drenched. She understood he was taking her to the rugby field. She felt an impulse to tell him to come under her umbrella, but she controlled herself. As they reached and stood exactly at the spot where they'd kissed, Tavish turned to look at her.

'I don't want to go in to why you didn't just grab me by my collar and tell me the truth when you understood that I was being an asshole but—'

'I don't like assholes,' Kisha interjected.

'Then tell me what you like. I'll be that way.'

Kisha stared at Tavish. She wanted to punch him hard and kiss him to death at the same time. She was pissed off with him as well as deeply in love with him. It took someone else telling him—Jas, Kisha guessed—for him to be convinced about her truth. Tavish stood waiting, getting drenched in the rain, awaiting a response from her. Meanwhile, her mind was clogged with several thoughts at once. The silence in-between told them how intensely they were into each other.

'Okay, we can stand here and gift ourselves pneumonia but—' Tavish couldn't complete his sentence as Kisha silenced him with a kiss. He held her hand and took charge of the umbrella as Kisha placed both her hands around his neck without breaking the kiss. As their tongues met, Tavish held the umbrella in a way that it covered both of them from prying eyes on campus. And one by one, the sound of the rain, the impact of the wind, the sense of where they were standing, all of it faded away in a supposed oblivion. What remained were two hearts beating in sync.

EIGHTEEN

TAVISH WALKED KISHA TO THE HOSTEL, BOTH UNDER THE umbrella, as the rain came down all around them. Neither talked, but both kept smiling at the other and looking into each other's eyes. Silence had never been so meaningful.

Kisha, lost in her sweet thoughts, entered her room. She could still feel Tavish's warm touch on her skin. The moment she locked her door, she noticed a sheet of paper hanging on the knob by a thread. She snatched it up and read it, snapping out of her reverie. As expected, the name of a book was written on it. So the Heartbreak Club members were establishing contact again. Kisha looked out of the window, the rain was still beating down hard. Kisha decided to wait for the morning rather than rush to the library right then.

When Kisha woke up, the rain had stopped and the morning looked fresh and clean. She sprang out of bed, changed out of her night dress into her uniform and dashed out to the library.

As Kisha entered the library, she glanced at the huge wall clock, that showed the time to be 7.15 a.m. She went to the computer section, found a free desktop and typed the name of the book that was written in the note. Knowing the coordinates, she went to the particular shelf and took it out. The book was slightly worn out and not in very good condition. Some of its pages were coming loose. Kisha carefully took the book and placed it on the table. Then, with a deep breath, she opened it. As she flipped through the pages, the highlighted words started appearing. By the time she reached the end, a meaningful phrase had formed: *One month gone do it in one week or get out.*

Kisha looked through the book to see if she had missed any more highlighted words but that was it. Closing the book, she sat there wondering what she should do next. She had feared something of this sort may happen. She had spent quite some time just gaining Ahaan's confidence but the truth was, her time as an exchange student was coming to an end soon. She had only two months and was sure the club members knew that. She sat there till she heard the bell for the morning assembly. As Kisha walked out of the library, she knew things were heating up.

In between classes, she met Tavish near the water cooler.

'They are asking me to complete my task within a week,' Kisha said. Tavish didn't ask her who they were or what the task was. He kept filling his water bottle. When it filled to the brim, Kisha turned the knob off. Tavish glanced at her. He looked like there was something on his mind and he was struggling to find the right words to say it.

'Spill it,' Kisha said, not able to handle the suspense.

'I think I should stay away from this,' Tavish said in a rush, then added, 'not you, but all this.'

Kisha was glad he added the last part. At least Tavish had clarity now.

'All this that has been happening—wooing Ahaan, seeking

the club members, pursuing Anara's truth—I don't have a problem with any of it. But I think it's for the best that I don't get involved in this. I love you and while I understand why you are doing what you are doing, it just messes with my head.'

Kisha nodded. Tavish was correct. Even though he had known her wooing Ahaan was fake, he hadn't been able to handle the repercussions of it. It had created misunderstandings between them that even Kisha hadn't foreseen. And now that they had managed to preserve their budding relationship in the nick of time, before it fell off the edge, she thought it was mature of Tavish to take a step back. And anyway, finding Anara's truth was always her pursuit, her battle. And people should fight their personal battles alone.

Kisha looked around. Confident they were alone, she held Tavish's hand.

'I understand. And thanks for being transparent about it. But...'

Their eyes held each other as he heard her say, 'Just be there.' Her grasp tightened. He held her back without looking around and said, 'Always, in all ways.'

Though Tavish had said he'd keep a distance from what Kisha was doing, he couldn't stop thinking about her and the danger she was putting herself in. Sometimes it's difficult to disconnect, even if one desires it. You are either into someone and their life completely, or you aren't. He had a class to attend but his mind was in a whirl, revolting against him. He decided to go for a quick swim instead.

Tavish was in the pool, completing his laps, when he spotted Vega eyeing him. Her presence irritated him, especially since he knew she'd been trying to cause misunderstandings between him and Kisha. He never understood why she kept pursuing him when he had given her no reason to. As Tavish moved out of the pool and started moving towards the shower area, he saw in the reflection of the mirrored wall in front, that Vega was recording him. That was it. He just snapped. Tavish marched up to her, snatched her phone away and started yelling.

'Who gave you the right to record me? Who gave you the right to record Kisha and Ahaan? Just because nobody complained doesn't mean you can continue your creepy behaviour!' There was a stunned silence in the entire swimming hall. Vega was taken aback. She had done this before too, recorded Tavish secretly and fawned over him in the privacy of her room. But he had never called her out.

'I'm ... I'm sorry but—'

'You better be sorry or else I'll make you sorry,' said Tavish and hurled the phone on the floor. It broke into three pieces. Everyone around was looking at them. Vega felt more humiliated than scared. If it was someone else, she would have definitely reacted, maybe even serving them a swift kick, but Tavish was a different entity for her. She thought she would apologise again, and had just opened her mouth, but was startled by Tavish grabbing the top of her swim suit to shake her. He was about to bellow further when everyone heard Kisha scream out Tavish's name.

Tavish and Vega turned together to see Kisha stomp towards them.

'Please, Tavish. This isn't proper,' she said. She held Tavish's hand and moved it away from Vega. Tavish knew she was right.

He moved away, casting a disgusted look at Vega, and hissed, 'Then explain it to her properly.' He went away to the shower room. Others too carried on with what they were up to, now that the show was over. Vega couldn't look Kisha in the eye.

'Thank you,' Vega said.

'There's a fine line between foolishness and losing your self-respect. And trust me, Vega, nobody can win one's love, or even lust, at the cost of self-respect,' Kisha said. She had all the abhorrence in her heart for what Vega had done, recording the kiss video, but that was for later. Here, she was talking to her as a girl.

Vega understood what Kisha meant. Not that she didn't know it already. Every time Tavish rejected her in a passive aggressive manner, she felt like she lost a chunk of her self-respect, and yet the next day she was back to doing the same. It was like she was addicted. Vega quietly picked up the pieces of her phone and left. Kisha went towards the shower room and waited for Tavish.

The moment Tavish emerged from the shower, he stopped, seeing Kisha.

'You're still here?'

'I wanted to talk to you before my classes began. What's going on, Tavish? Why so much anger? Trust me, I've done stupid things and have my own anger issues but this could land you in serious trouble.'

'I know it wasn't right of me to hold her like that. I'm sorry. But ...'

Kisha sensed Tavish was avoiding eye contact.

'But what?' she urged.

'I'm feeling terrible that I can't help you in any way about Anara.'

When Kisha realised what it was that was actually eating up Tavish from the inside, she could have kissed him then and there.

'Tavish, calm down. It's my battle. Even if we love each other we have to fight our battles ourselves. And I respect you for thinking this way but I'll have to do it alone. You have to trust me.'

'Promise me if you need any help, you won't think twice about asking me.'

Kisha held his hand and said, 'I promise.'

After all that drama, the rest of the day passed rather uneventfully. Kisha did meet Ahaan outside class, but apart from a casual chat and him giving her another reversible sketch, nothing more happened. In her room, as she was placing the reversible sketch in a drawer where she had kept all of Ahaan's sketches, she held the image upside down, only to realise it was an image of a boy with a birthday crown from one angle and without from another. *Was that a hint?* Kisha didn't have to think long as her phone buzzed with a message: *May I come to your room?* It was Ahaan. Kisha called him.

'What happened?'

'It's my birthday tomorrow and I want to be with the best person I know at midnight.'

Ah, thus the sketch, Kisha thought. She said, 'But it's so late. Coming here will be damn risky. What if we get caught—'

'Leave that to me,' Ahaan said and disconnected. He had never sounded so confident ever before.

Half an hour before midnight, there were a few urgent knocks at the door. Kisha opened the door to see Jas standing there, with another girl whom she had not met before.

'She wanted to meet you. Okay bye,' Jas said simply, as she pushed the girl inside and pulled the main door shut. Kisha was a bit taken aback and eyed the girl, who looked very familiar. Kisha slowly realised where she had seen her... and clasped her palm to her mouth. Ahaan smiled at her, taking off his wig. Kisha was amazed at his transformation.

'Don't be so shocked. I always win top spot at dramatics, remember?' Ahaan said with a gleeful laugh. He was correct. She knew that about his dramatics but she hadn't seen him perform before.

For the next half hour, they watched Netflix together on her tab and chit chatted. Ahaan kept telling her more about him. Little things he hadn't told her before. His passion for the arts and how when he'd told his parents about it, they had thought he was gay. How he was sick of people making fun of those who aren't alphas. How he believed there was no one way to be a man. Kisha kept listening to him. She didn't know Ahaan could make so much sense. Or perhaps she was so used to looking at him as a means to get to the Heartbreak Club, that she had never tried to get to know the person that he was.

As the clock was about to strike midnight—only two minutes to go—Ahaan paused the show they were watching on the tab and looked at her.

'Kisha, I'd a wish for my eighteenth birthday.'

Kisha understood something awkward was about to come out.

'What is it?' she asked hesitantly.

'I want someone to see me naked. And that someone should

be someone I love. I know I'm not perfect, but baring yourself in front of someone you love, and witnessing how they see you, gives you the strength to accept your own shame,' Ahaan said. There was an arresting genuineness about him. She observed Ahaan get up from bed and take few steps away from her. He started stripping. Kisha didn't know what to do. She definitely did not want to see Ahaan naked, but she didn't know what to tell him. She knew Ahaan's wish wasn't motivated by lust. It was way more personal and deeper. He wanted to feel loved and appreciated. As he took his tee off, Kisha noticed his ribs poking out. She wasn't surprised. She had seen him during their swimming session. He was unbelievably thin.

Ahaan's phone buzzed with an alarm. It was midnight. His birthday. Ahaan held his lowers and was about to tug it down when Kisha stopped him on an impulse.

'Your intention isn't wrong, Ahaan,' Kisha said, 'but I think you should look at me, and through my eyes know you are beautiful in your own way. You don't have to disrobe. The fact that you have been fighting the deep-seated insecurities about your self, makes you a fighter. And fighters can never be ugly.'

Ahaan had tears in his eyes.

'Happy birthday. One should never cry on this day,' Kisha said in a gentle manner.

Ahaan hugged Kisha and whispered in her ears, 'Thank you for saying what you did. You don't know how important it was for me that you didn't react the way others do.'

They remained in the platonic embrace for some time. For Ahaan it was a dream he was living out. Kisha didn't stop him, for she could sense it was important for him. It wasn't sexual intimacy, still, Kisha was alert. She wanted to be careful. One step and she would be cheating on Tavish. She held herself tight but nothing more happened. Ahaan broke the hug, wore his clothes and went away in another fifteen minutes, disguised in his wig.

Kisha sat down on her bed with a thud. This was the moment. Whatever happened in the room told her that Ahaan was irreversibly in love with her now. And this was the moment when she had to begin the 'damaging Ahaan' part. She controlled her emotions which were telling her to stop, to not hurt him, while her determination to know what had happened to Anara made her open a shopping app on her phone. She typed into the search bar: *Fake tattoo*. It was time for Kisha to become something she had never thought she would ever become: a villain in someone's life.

NINETEEN

AHAAN WAS SURPRISED WHEN A CAKE WAS BROUGHT INTO the class with his name on it. This had never happened before. The teacher conducting the class announced that it was sent by his parents, but Ahaan was not convinced. He would be surprised if they even remembered his birthday, leave aside sending a cake. The teacher asked Ahaan to cut the cake in front of everyone, which he did despite his crippling shyness. He stole furtive glances at Kisha who was smiling at him while clapping and singing for him, like everyone else. Ahaan had never been happier.

When the class was over, Kisha went up to him and said, 'Happy birthday!'

'Thanks. Though I don't believe my parents sent me the cake for a second,' he said, beaming.

'How does it matter who sent it. It was sent with love, and that's what's important.'

Ahaan tried to read through the twinkle in Kisha's eyes.

'Thank you for last night. I couldn't sleep because of my happiness. I think it will remain the most important birthday eve of my life till I'm alive.'

'My mum says one shouldn't be talking of death on birthdays.'

'Sorry,' he said with a smile, as the two collected their things and made their way to the next class.

Tavish, while walking towards the rugby field with his team mates, noticed Vega cycling to the library. He ran towards her and surprised her by stepping in her way and stopping her.

'I'm sorry, Vega. I shouldn't have touched you,' Tavish said. His conversation with Kisha had stayed with him. And he had no qualms about apologising for doing something wrong. Touching a girl without permission wasn't something he would want himself to repeat.

'It's okay,' Vega said and shrugged.

'I lost my temper and it wasn't cool, but I hope you understand why I was angry. I know what you feel for me. I'm not a toddler.'

'I'm glad you do.' Vega was holding her ground this time, unlike the last time when she was too taken aback to speak up.

'But as you know, it's not necessary for me to reciprocate what you feel. I hope you can respect that.'

Vega was fighting hard to supress her tears. She didn't want to cry in front of him. After the showdown, she had promised herself that she would slowly but surely come out of the spell that Tavish had cast on her since the time she had laid eyes on him, a few years ago. Even though she had no idea how she would do it. Maybe, she wondered, she would do it by putting into practice the favourite concept of adults: moving on.

'I get it. I'm getting late now. Please do excuse me,' Vega said and continued on her way towards the library. Tavish was looking at her retreating form, when he realised there was a presence beside him. He turned to see Jas.

'Leave her alone. She has finally understood the impossible.'

Tavish smiled at Jas. If there was one person who had equal access to both the boys' and the girls' hostel, it was Jas. She wasn't exactly a tomboy but the majority of her friends were boys.

'Yeah,' Tavish said. One of his teammates called out to him to join them. Tavish waved at them, signalling that he would be there in a minute. He faced Jas and said, 'It's good I met you here.'

Jas raised a single eyebrow, wondering what he meant exactly.

'I need a favour. I want some things smuggled inside the girls' hostel tonight.'

'Go on, I'm listening.'

While Tavish told Jas his plan, which was to be executed later that night, Ahaan took Kisha, after classes were over for the day, to the under-construction swimming pool area. The air was heavy with moisture.

'Don't you think we should be indoors? It looks like it may rain any minute,' Kisha asked wiping the sweat off her forehead.

'I wanted us to be away from prying eyes,' Ahaan said.

'For?'

'You'll find out soon.'

As the two reached the spot, Kisha noticed a small table with a red cloth spread on it. Ahaan quickly approached the table, took out a fragrant candle and lit it.

'I'm sorry I couldn't arrange the chairs,' he said. It was clear he was trying to pull off some sort of an in-premise date. 'But

I got this for you.' Ahaan took out two boxes of frozen French vanilla from the newly opened Tim Hortons. Kisha found his effort and excitement very cute but didn't let on. Suddenly she realised it was her turn to say something.

'Amazing. This is the first time I'll have Tim Hortons in India.' She smiled.

Ahaan beamed saying, 'I was hoping that was the case. When you do something for the first time with someone, you not only remember that something but that someone as well.'

Kisha nodded happily, not making it evident that she was noting the subtle way he was making his feelings further clear. Ahaan gallantly opened the boxes and they started to have the ice cream, standing by the table.

'Delicious, but it wasn't necessary you know,' Kisha said.

'Nor was the cake,' Ahaan said.

'That was your parents!'

'Oh, come on! I may be a nerd but I'm not stupid, Kisha,' Ahaan said. He saw Kisha's sheepish expression and grinned.

Kisha realised she had underestimated Ahaan. He was, after all, the class topper. It wasn't easy to keep things from him.

'Well, I've something to show you as well,' Kisha said, seizing on the moment.

Ahaan looked at her expectantly.

It was time for her to take this to next level. Kisha folded the sleeve of her shirt a little, and revealed the skin around her elbow. Ahaan could see the letter 'A' tattooed just above her elbow. He looked at her, incredulous. Did the 'A' stand for him and not Anara? It had to be, why else would Kisha show it to him. But Ahaan found the entire thing too fantastical to be real. Was Kisha this crazy about him? She had never given him a clue. On the other hand, if he had tattooed 'K' on his arm, it would have made sense, considering how much he worshipped her. Kisha was happy Ahaan appreciated the tattoo and did not seem to realise it was fake.

The night before, after seeing how hopelessly in love Ahaan was with her, Kisha gave everything a long thought. There were two options for her. Either do what THC wanted and pass the test. That would mean she would get into the club and figure out what had happened to Anara. Or the other option was to just let it all go. She checked Anara's phone gallery. Her phone had been handed over to Prithibi, who had passed it on to Kisha.

As she went through her sister's photos, Kisha contemplated. She didn't even know who had sent her the anonymous message based on which she had come all the way to India. But that could be figured out later. First, what did she want? Letting her mind wander aimlessly for an hour, Kisha understood she hadn't reached that emotional stage yet where she could let it all go. She was not ready to accept things. She needed to know what had happened to her sister, and for that if she had to get a fake tattoo to make Ahaan believe he was in love with her, she would.

While Kisha was having ice cream with Ahaan, Jas was quickly putting whatever Tavish had asked her to in her room. Jas had stolen Kisha's room keys from her bag. Tavish had sent soft toys, books, wind chimes, scented candles ... everything that Kisha loved. He had blown up a picture of Kisha from her Instagram and framed it. That, too, was placed on her desk. Finally, Jas pinned the large poster above Kisha's study table.

It had the back of two lovers sitting side by side, admiring a sunrise on a mountain. A line was written under the image: *We are each other's.*

Below it, Tavish had written *T hearts K*. Once she was done, Jas moved out of the room and locked it. Her plan was to find Kisha and tell her she had found the room keys in their class. Of course, once she entered the room she would know the truth. And she wouldn't mind Jas' thievery one bit. Jas was sure of it.

Just when they'd finished their ice creams, it started pouring. Kisha and Ahaan took refuge under the tree, waiting for the rain to subside. There was a sudden shift of energy between them which was palpable. Before this, they had been laughing and joking, enjoying their ice creams. Now, silence and a sharp awareness of their proximity, as they stood sheltering from the rain, overtook them.

Kisha was reminded of the rugby field, where she and Tavish had shared a kiss. It was raining then, it was raining now. She suddenly missed Tavish, and wished she was standing here with him instead. He wasn't part of her personal battle and it was something she had agreed to and yet, it felt wrong to not share whatever was happening in her life with him. With every passing second her craving for Tavish kept ascending. She wanted to call him then and there, but she knew she had to move away from Ahaan to do so. She decided to tell Ahaan that she would brave the rain and run to the hostel. The moment she turned, Ahaan surprised her by holding her by the waist and planting a peck on her cheeks. He then looked at her but her eyes were closed.

'Now we can kiss, right?' he asked.

In that moment everything that had been on her mind, started flashing in front of Kisha's eyes. Anara, the notes from THC, Tavish, their intimacy, their fight, their kiss, the rugby field … Kisha opened her eyes. Driven by an impulse, she pushed Ahaan. He lost his balance and toppled over while she ran into the rain. She wasn't crying but she wanted to hide. From herself. She had made up her mind that she would go with what the club wanted her to do, after such careful thought, and all it took was a peck, a simple peck, from Ahaan to make her realise what an idiot she was being. Midway, her phone rang. Kisha saw it was Jas. She kept running till she reached the girls' hostel; all drenched. Jas was standing in the lobby.

'You dropped your—' Jas said, dangling the keys in front of Kisha. Kisha simply snatched it from her and ran up the stairs to her room. When she entered and shut the door behind her, she stood still, looking all around her, amazed. It was as if she had stepped into a different room. Her eyes went to the poster above her study. And the line written on it. Then on the '*T hearts K*'. She walked up to it, gently running her fingers over the letters. It's now that her tears welled up as she murmured to herself, 'I love you, Tavish Mathur. And this can't go on. Not like this. I'll end it with Ahaan.'

TWENTY

KISHA KNEW THE MORE SHE WAITED, THE MORE CONFUSION it would cause in her mind. In twenty-four hours, she had actually changed her mind completely twice. First, when she decided to continue to pursue the mystery behind Anara's disappearance, and second when she realised she couldn't keep up the farce with Ahaan and decided to give it all up for Tavish. After calming herself with a few deep breaths, Kisha called Ahaan from her phone.

Tavish completed his swim practice and came out of the club to see it was still raining. As he stood under the concrete canopy of the building, he noticed Kisha walking towards him, holding an umbrella. He wondered if she had come there especially, since it was raining. And to thank him for the efforts he had made in decorating her room. He had been waiting for her call, once Jas told him she had arrived and gone to her room. But none came. Kisha reached him, closed the umbrella and glanced around. Because of the rain there was nobody there.

'We need to talk,' she said. The seriousness in her voice told Tavish that something was wrong.

'What happened?' he asked.

Kisha averted her gaze, as if trying to collect her thoughts, and then looked into Tavish's eyes and said, 'I confessed to Ahaan.'

―◦

When Kisha called Ahaan, he answered eagerly, despite what had just happened between them. She didn't say much, only asked him to meet her behind the girls' hostel. She walked up to their designated meeting spot and saw Ahaan already there, smiling at her uncertainly. Perhaps he thought she had come to explain her behaviour. Kisha stood in front of him and said, 'Just forget whatever happened between us in the past few weeks.'

'What do you mean? You can't be that angry. I'm sorry, I know I should have taken permission to give you a peck.'

Kisha rolled her eyes and said, 'Ahaan, this isn't about the peck.' She swallowed. She knew she owed him some of the truth, if not the entire truth.

'I only pursued you because I was asked to do so.'

Ahaan frowned. 'What are you talking about?'

'Trust me, I can't tell you everything. Just understand that I was asked to make you fall in love with me and then break your heart. I overestimated myself. I thought I'd be able to do it but as I got to know you, I realised you have your own vulnerabilities too and it wasn't fair. But most importantly …' This was the most difficult part Kisha had to admit to. 'I'm in love with Tavish. Maybe too deeply to even woo another guy, even if it's fake.'

There was silence. Ahaan neither said anything nor did he look at Kisha. He was looking into the distance, his eyes glazed, his lips pursed.

'I know it's my fault. And I am sorry to have misled you. I'm okay being friends but …' Kisha didn't have to say the rest. Ahaan simply turned and walked away with stooped shoulders. Kisha felt miserable. She knew he loved her. Genuinely. But she, too, was helpless. The only thing she took heart in was that she'd confessed to him before it was too late. Before she had to break his heart. That would have been the point of no return. A sheer disaster.

Standing in front of Tavish now, she relayed to him whatever she'd told Ahaan. Tavish's face lit up with happiness. It meant they were now free to live out their love story. But then something else struck him.

'So, does that mean you won't pursue the truth behind Anara's disappearance?'

'Anara Di's disappearance was what brought me here. But I didn't anticipate that I would meet someone and fall in love.'

Tavish touched her face gently.

Kisha continued. 'Now that I have, things are no longer simple. I was confident of making Ahaan fall in love with me. Maybe he already is. But when I accepted the black handshake, I didn't fully realise the repercussions it would have. Especially on me as a person and my personal choices. Now I do. And I'm not ready to compromise my present.' She touched Tavish's jawline and added, 'Not even an inch.'

Tavish leaned forward so that his forehead touched hers. The tips of their noses also touched. Their lips brushed against each other's.

'Thanks, Kisha,' Tavish said. 'You don't know what a weight has been lifted off my chest. Even though I told you that I won't be involved in your personal battle, but deep inside it was killing me.'

'I know,' Kisha said, recollecting the conversation they had had outside the shower room.

They hugged tight. The rain intensified. Tavish smiled. Kisha broke the hug and shrugged.

'It was raining the first time we kissed. It is raining now too. Perhaps nature is a witness to the purity of our love,' he said.

Kisha hadn't heard anything more beautiful than that. She held his hand and pulled him inside the swimming club. Tavish knew where she was taking him. They entered the empty shower room and closed the door. Kisha pushed Tavish against the door and started smooching him passionately.

'Dare you leave me, ever,' Kisha said.

Tavish smirked and said, 'Dare you think I'll leave you, ever.'

Kisha returned to the girl's hostel once the rain had subsided. She felt light and happy. After days of confusion, there was finally some clarity. It was as if the confession to Ahaan had swept away all her fears and the dilemma with it. She smiled to herself. She video called her mother, who she hadn't spoken to in a while. She found Ranya sounding much better than before. While talking, her mother divulged how she had come to the realisation that Prithibi leaving had in fact been a good thing. She had always found his presence oppressive, even if she hadn't admitted it to herself. She was able to breathe now and live a life that she enjoyed. Earlier, she had been living her life on the periphery, always privileging Prithibi's career, his decisions. Ranya said, she had realised that in every love story, while it was romantic to lose yourself, it was also important to maintain your individuality. When she had checked in with herself, she found her emotional side ailing. Prithibi's going away was the much-needed medicine, even though she had initially felt otherwise.

After speaking to her mum, Kisha changed out of her wet clothes to something comfortable. She was about to settle in for the night, when she received a phone call from Ahaan. She picked it up after hesitating for some time.

'Yes, Ahaan?'

'Can we meet now?'

'I don't think it's a good idea.'

'It's important, trust me.'

'Can we video call please?'

'Yeah, that should work.'

Ahaan switched the audio call to a video one. He appeared on screen. Kisha noticed he was inside a room, probably his own, with a study table behind him.

'Thanks for confessing to me today, Kisha,' Ahaan said. Kisha managed a tight smile. She didn't want him to go on an emotional trip right now. She was in a good space mentally, enjoying her peace of mind after a long while.

'I too have to confess something.'

Kisha looked at him uncertainly. Ahaan had never sounded this serious before.

'What is it?'

'I know why you were trying to make me fall in love with you.'

Kisha frowned, trying to understand if he was lying to get back at her.

'Is that so? Why?' she asked.

'The Heartbreak Club members asked you to. I was your black handshake.'

For a moment, Kisha felt someone had knocked the air out of her. How on earth could Ahaan know this? Unless ...

'I'm the Bishop. And though I knew what you were doing, loving you wasn't a game for me. I know you want to figure out what happened to Anara. And I can still help you with it,' Ahaan said in a matter of fact manner.

Kisha's eyes widened in shock. It wasn't even funny how the whole situation had boomeranged back into her life. She was talking to one of the members of the club! She was suddenly full of questions. She wanted to ask him about THC, about being the Bishop. She wanted to know if he was serious or kidding. Some truths sound so ridiculous that you have a hard time believing them at first. She sighed and said, 'How can you help me, Ahaan?'

'I can act like I've gone mad because you broke my heart. I can even be away from school for a month. By then you can gain entry to the club. And once you're in, even if I return to Fairmont High completely sane, no one will throw you out.'

The proposal was totally alluring. No loop holes. But the thing with alluring proposals was that they were almost never free.

'What's the catch?' Kisha asked. Ahaan smirked. A most discomfiting smirk.

'You break up with Tavish.' A pause later he added, 'Not a fake break up, mind you.'

Kisha had slapped Ahaan before. This time she would have punched him if he had been in front of her.

TWENTY-ONE

THE VIDEO CALL ENDED ABRUPTLY, BUT KISHA'S EXPRESSIONS had already conveyed to Ahaan that he had thrown her in the middle of a storm of confusion. Sleep was a far cry that night. The funny thing about Ahaan's proposal was that it was pulling her strongly in two opposite directions. On one hand he had offered something which she had been trying very hard to do—get into THC to know Anara's truth. On the other hand, he was asking for something she could never imagine in her wildest dreams, leave alone in reality—breaking up with Tavish. She thought hard but there was no middle ground in the proposal, no room for negotiation.

The next day, right after breakfast, she met Tavish by the rugby field. Kisha had messaged him in the morning asking him to meet, and by the time she reached, Tavish was already there.

'Ahaan is the Bishop,' Kisha declared, without preamble. Tavish didn't understand immediately, but when he did, his jaw fell open. Kisha took couple of minutes to tell him what had transpired the night before. By the time she was done, Tavish looked as flabbergasted as her.

'I've been in this school for eleven years now and what the grapevine suggests is that the club started twenty years back. This is the first time a member has exposed himself.'

'Okay. What are you trying to say?'

'It's obvious, isn't it? This is all hogwash. How do we know Ahaan is the bishop? Just because he said so? Well, I can say I'm the King, you the Queen. How does it matter?'

'So, what are you suggesting?'

'Ask him to prove that he is the Bishop.'

Kisha thought about it for a moment.

'And what if he does prove it? I can't—' Kisha couldn't bear to complete the sentence.

Tavish knew what she was thinking. She had just decided to choose him over the club, and now this. It was an emotional rollercoaster.

'Well, if he is going to pretend to be crazy, why can't we pretend to break up?'

'No, no, no,' Kisha said and marched ahead of Tavish. She turned around, looking stricken. 'I can't get into that cycle again where we act fake and then our reality suffers,' Kisha said and felt Tavish's hand on her shoulder.

'Let Ahaan prove it first. I think it's a great counter to his proposal. If he is lying then there's no question of you considering his condition. And if he is saying the truth, we at least get to know one of the five THC members. Don't you think that itself could lead you further in?'

Kisha nodded.

Sitting in class, Kisha was lost in her thoughts. She had no idea what the teacher was saying. All she could do was glance at Ahaan. He was listening to the teacher and making diligent notes. He didn't look at her even once. Tavish's words kept playing in her mind. She hadn't thought of the whole situation from that angle. Would Ahaan lie about something like that? It was a great bait, she had to agree. But, clearly there was more to him than he had previously let on. He had known that THC made her woo him and yet he hadn't shot down her proposal. He definitely knew more than she did. Suddenly something else struck her, the night when Selena had called her near the under-construction swimming pool area, someone else had been there who had hurt her. Ahaan had appeared out of nowhere right after that. Was it him who had hit her? It was impossible to tell. But if it was really him, then his pretense was of a standard that could be labelled psychopathic.

The class got over. Kisha kept an eye on Ahaan. She had always thought he was a loner. Now she noticed him more closely. He had no friends. People only talked to him when they had some academic issues. Could such a boy be part of THC? But then again, how would she know what kind of people they roped in? After all, they had offered her a chance to get in as well and she was certainly not the most popular kid around. Or, was it that this whole thing was a sham? Nobody in the club knew about the black handshake and it was simply Ahaan who had concocted the whole drama? There was only one person who could answer all her questions.

'Ahaan!' Kisha shouted. Ahaan, who was on his way out of the class, stopped, but didn't turn. He knew it was Kisha. He waited till Kisha came up from behind and turned to stand face to face with him.

'Yes, Kisha?' His demeanor had definitely undergone a change since his confession. The most distinct was his confidence of which she hadn't even had a glimpse before.

'I accept your condition,' Kisha said.

The slight smile on Ahaan's face told Kisha that he had expected her to accept his proposal.

'But, I too have a condition,' she continued.

'Counter-condition? Interesting. And what may that be?' Ahaan asked. Kisha did notice he was looking at her eyes, arrow-straight, and talking. Something which he didn't do before.

'You have to prove to me that you're the bishop. I mean, too much is at stake and I need to know you aren't lying.'

Ahaan was quiet, but his eyes were studying Kisha. It was as if he was weighing if she was tricking him into anything.

'Alright,' he said at last. 'I'll prove it.'

Kisha felt a knot in her stomach. His conviction was conclusive. She didn't know what scared her, that she felt he would prove it to her or what would happen if he *did* prove it.

'By when?'

'Tomorrow,' Ahaan said.

'I'll wait.'

'But you remember the deal, right? Once I prove I'm the Bishop, there's no turning back. You'll have to break up with Tavish.'

Kisha only nodded in agreement. Ahaan walked away. There was a subtle swag in his walk, delusion of grandeur that she hadn't noticed before. Was she imagining it because now there was a possibility that he could be the Bishop? Kisha wasn't sure.

Kisha met Tavish at the school café. He was with Surya. The moment Kisha appeared, Surya left. Kisha told Tavish about what Ahaan had told her.

'So, the little runt is playing it tough.'

'He is. Looking at him, I don't think he is kidding.'

'You mean he indeed is the Bishop?'

'So, I feel.'

'Here's a plan. If he proves to you that he is the bishop, then we will corner him and make him cough up who the others in the group are.'

'How will you corner him?'

'Leave that to me. That nincompoop will blurt out everything if I catch him by his balls. Assuming he has balls,' Tavish said with a snarl.

'Tavish, please. Let's not be nasty. He has had his issues. I don't know whether he made it up or not but I don't want to judge his weakness on the basis of his involvement with the Heartbreak Club.'

'Alright, alright. Topic change. I was thinking of something else as well.'

'What?'

'You have only a month to go back to London, right?'

Kisha had consciously tried to avoid thinking about her impending departure. But avoiding it didn't mean it would go away. She had to address it sooner or later.

'I know.' Kisha almost choked on her words.

'Hey, don't be upset. That's what I wanted to talk about. I've six more months to go before I pass out. And I've already started applying to universities in the UK for my undergrad.'

Kisha could have kissed him right then. He hadn't come to her with a problem. He'd found a solution and had put it in action as well.

'I love you.'

'I love you too,' Tavish said clasping her hand.

'It's just six months. That's manageable I guess.'

'Knowing we will live together after six months, makes it more than manageable,' Kisha said with a smile.

That night Kisha couldn't sleep. She was wondering how Ahaan would prove he was indeed the Bishop. Her thoughts drifted to who might have started the Heartbreak Club. What was its agenda? How could they have continued to run in the school for so long? Kisha didn't realise when her thoughts lulled her to sleep.

The next morning, the moment she reached her class, she looked for Ahaan but he wasn't there. He didn't appear during the next class either. Nor during the last class. And when Kisha called Tavish that evening to check in the boys' hostel, there was a slight fear in his voice when he answered.

'Kisha, there is some bad news. Ahaan is nowhere to be found.'

TWENTY-TWO

'WHAT DO YOU MEAN NOWHERE TO BE FOUND?' KISHA'S fear had made her voice brittle.

'I checked everywhere. He has not been seen in the hostel since last night. Nor did he go to class. The boy has vanished.'

Vanished! Like Anara did. Kisha could feel the fear churn within her. She sat down. Had Ahaan met with the same fate as Anara? Kisha had a bad feeling about it all.

'We have to report this to the authorities,' she found herself say.

'Yeah, warden sir has already been told. And he has informed Dr Iyer. He is coming to the hostel right now. I'll keep you posted on what happens. And let's not tell anything of what Ahaan told you. I don't want you to be roped into all this.'

'Yeah, sure. I understand.' Kisha ended the call. That's when she realised that she was shivering violently. She slipped into bed, ensconced inside the blanket. The shivers subsided eventually, but guilt surfaced. Had Ahaan vanished because of her? The Heartbreak Club kept a watch on everything, they must've discovered that Ahaan had confessed to being the Bishop. Or maybe when Ahaan was trying to prove that he was indeed the Bishop, someone from the club had come to know. He would prove it in one day, Ahaan had said. And that one day had proved to be—Kisha dreaded to even think of the word—fatal. The realisation that nothing of that sort would have happened if she hadn't accepted the black handshake, was slowly suffocating her. Her only redemption would be if Ahaan came back or was found in an unharmed state. And that too soon.

⸺

Dr Iyer came to the boys' hostel. The warden had briefed him about what had happened. The students were asked to gather in the lobby. Dr Iyer stood looking at them and asked, 'Who saw Ahaan last?' Nobody said anything till one student raised a tentative hand. He was a junior studying in standard nine.

'Sir … I saw him leave the hostel last night, around midnight.'

'What were you doing outside your room at midnight?' Dr Iyer shot back.

'I … I had come down to fill my water bottle from the cooler. My room's cooler hasn't been functioning for a few days now,' the student stammered.

Dr Iyer looked at the warden and asked, 'What does Ahaan's log say?'

The students were supposed to log their movements on the school's hostel app, if they had to move out of the hostel, even within the school campus, after 7 p.m. The silence that followed from the warden told Dr Iyer the obvious. The warden clearly hadn't kept a log of it. He gave the warden a stern glance and made a mental note of talking to him about the carelessness later when alone.

'Did you call his phone?' Dr Iyer said.

The warden immediately spoke up this time. 'I did, Sir. Several times. But his phone is switched off.'

Dr Iyer thought for some time and then said aloud to the students in the lobby.

'Please don't panic. I'll inform the police. Please cooperate with them. And of course, Ahaan's parents will be told right away.' He turned to the warden and said in a low tone, 'Meet me in my cabin in ten minutes.' He walked out, leaving behind a cacophony of voices amongst the students.

The morning that followed was chaotic. There was a heaviness in the air and a certain eeriness. Everyone knew what had happened but no one was talking about it openly. When Kisha came out of her hostel, she noticed a couple of police vans outside the academic building. The warden of the girls' hostel had already told them, during their breakfast, that the police may talk to some of them and they'd need to cooperate. She had also said that their parents had been informed about what had transpired.

When Kisha reached the academic building, Tavish joined her.

'It's just chaos. There are two police officers, one male and one female, who are interrogating students about Ahaan.'

Kisha's fear reflected on her face when she heard about the police. What would she tell them if they asked her about Ahaan's disappearance?

'Did they ask you anything?' Kisha spoke to Tavish.

He shook his head and said, 'Not yet, because nothing connects me to him. But I have a feeling they may interrogate you. Surya told me your name came up during some of the students' interrogation.'

'Okay,' she said, feeling that nothing was okay. She saw a familiar person coming out of the academic building. It was her father, she noted with surprise.

'What are you doing here, dad?' Kisha ran up to him and said. Despite her complicated relationship with him, she was glad he was here. Prithibi glanced at Tavish, and then looked at Kisha. 'The police had called me. Apparently, another student from your school has disappeared. Someone named Ahaan Rawat. You knew him?' he said.

'He was in my batch.'

'Right. I had to sign the consent letter so they could ask you questions. Also, the police called me as they wanted to know if Anara knew him. The last person to disappear like this was—'

'Anara di,' Kisha completed.

'Yes. Anyway, I'll have to go now. Have this super urgent meeting. Call me if you need anything, okay?' Prithibi said, glancing at his cell phone.

'Call me if you need anything?' Was that the extent of parental responsibility? Kisha thought. Aloud she put up a brave front and said, 'Sure, dad.'

Prithibi patted her cheek and left.

'Wow. Are all parents the same these days?' Tavish commented. Kisha gave a dejected shrug and said, 'I'll have to go to class now. I'll let you know if they call me.'

'Cool. You take care.'

Soon enough, Kisha was summoned for questioning. The police personnel had taken over a room to question people. She entered it and looked around. She noticed there were a few more people in the room, apart from the police and the counsellor. There were two cops, one woman and one man, both in uniform. Their uniform was the same, so were the number of stars on their shoulder strap. Kisha concluded they must be of the same rank. She was asked to sit on a chair opposite everyone else present in the room.

The female police officer stood up and went around her chair and placed her hands on Kisha's shoulders. 'Please relax. This is just a routine enquiry. I'm Pallavi, leading this case and Anara Sen's case's investigation. That's Mr and Mrs Rawat, Ahaan's parents,' she said.

Kisha glanced at them. They didn't look like a couple who would be volatile at home. But then, Kisha told herself, these things were seldom apparent, which is what made it more sinister.

'And that's Officer Mitesh Kalia.'

Kisha nodded at the male officer as a mark of greeting.

'And that's Dr Juneja. You know her, of course. She is your school counsellor. We can't question students without her being here.'

'Just relax, Kisha,' Dr Juneja said. 'As Officer Pallavi said it's just routine enquiry since one of your batchmates has suddenly disappeared. If any question of theirs makes you uncomfortable, please say so. And you don't have to answer it either.'

'Okay, doctor.' Kisha said. She saw Officer Pallavi go back to her seat.

'Anara Sen was your elder sister, right?'

'That's correct, ma'am.'

'I'm asking because we had come to this school when she had disappeared too. Unfortunately, she hasn't been found still, but the case is open. I think you weren't in the school at the time.'

'No ma'am. I was in rehab, in London.'

'Rehab? What for?' Officer Pallavi asked.

'Anger management issues,' Kisha said and immediately realised she'd said too much. She should simply have said that she was studying in London, at the time.

'I see. You know that one of your batch mates has disappeared?'

'Yes, I heard.'

'It's not yet twenty-four hours since Ahaan went missing. Usually, we wait for twenty-four hours for someone to be tagged missing. But this is slightly different, since something similar did happen around eight months back. That too in Fairmont.' There was a pause and then Officer Pallavi said, 'That time it was your sister, Anara.'

Kisha licked her lips anxiously. She hoped she wasn't looking as nervous as she was feeling.

'How well did you know Ahaan Rawat?' Officer Pallavi asked.

'As much as I know any other batch mate.'

'Is that so? But I got to know that you were his girlfriend?'

Kisha had never felt her heart beating so hard ever before.

TWENTY-THREE

'WHOEVER TOLD YOU THAT I WAS AHAAN'S GIRLFRIEND, perhaps doesn't know the difference between friendship and love,' Kisha said. She noticed Officer Pallavi raise her eyebrows and smirk.

'How thick were you as friends?'

'Well, I've only been here five months. We weren't besties, but somehow Ahaan used to tell me things which I believe he never told anyone.' This time Kisha was quick with her answer. She had already been caught lying once. She would have to regain Officer Pallavi's trust.

'Such as?'

Kisha's eyes darted towards Officer Mitesh and Dr Juneja. The therapist understood it was her que to speak.

'Is there a problem, Kisha?'

'Ma'am, whatever Ahaan told me about himself was in strict confidence. I don't feel right about mentioning it here.'

'I understand, Kisha, but we only have Ahaan's parents here and the police. Nothing will go beyond this room. You have my word. And theirs too.' Dr Juneja looked around. 'It's just that you never know what could be linked to his disappearance. Anything you tell us may help.' Dr Juneja's last statement sent a shiver down Kisha's spine. That was it. He indeed had disappeared because of what he shared with her. Or so Kisha concluded in her mind.

'Fine. He told me he still wets his pants at times. And that's because he grew up in a household where violence between his parents, and at times towards him, was the norm. It gave him serious anxiety issues.'

Kisha glanced at Ahaan's parents. The same couple who had till then been sitting there with furrowed brows and tearful expressions, suddenly looked visibly uncomfortable. They didn't seem to know what to do or say. And to Kisha, their silence just validated what Ahaan had told her.

'This is untrue. He never did anything of that sort at home,' Mrs Rawat spoke up at last. The lack of conviction in her voice was so evident that nobody responded. Officer Pallavi fixed her gaze on Kisha.

'Did anything happen between you two which may have triggered Ahaan's disappearance?' she asked.

This was the moment of truth for Kisha. If she told them what she thought was the reason for his disappearance, a lot of things would be compromised. Including her pursuit of Anara.

'We weren't that close, that anything I said or did would affect him enough to disappear. And even if we had been, I don't think anything happened between us which may have triggered it,' Kisha said. In her mind, she swore to herself that while she had lied to keep her pursuit of her elder sister going, she would also now look for Ahaan. She wouldn't rest in peace till she learnt whatever had happened to him and Anara. She noticed the two police officers exchange glances. Then, Officer Pallavi looked at her and said, 'That's it, Miss Sen. We will let you know if we need to ask you anything else later.'

'Sure, ma'am,' Kisha said and walked out of the room, her breathing unnaturally fast. As she walked out of the makeshift interrogation room, she knew exactly where she was going next. To the library. She entered, picked out the last book which the club had used to communicate with her, and sat with it on an adjacent table. She intentionally took a green marker. The Heartbreak Club used yellow to highlight words. Then, she sat and started marking words in a random sequence: What. Happened. To. Ahaan. Tell me. Else. Going. To. Mention THC. To. Them. Next.

Kisha closed the book, slipped it back on the shelf, and walked out of the library. She knew it was a shot in the dark. There was no way she could tell the club that she had written a message for them in the book. But her gut said she was under their radar. Not only now, but from the time she had started pursuing the mystery behind Anara's disappearance.

Nothing else happened during the day. Kisha couldn't meet Tavish because he was busy with his practice for an upcoming inter school rugby competition. He called her at night from his room.

'So sorry, I couldn't meet you during the day. What did the police say?'

Kisha had been waiting to hear from Tavish. As soon as she heard his voice, she felt a sense of calm. She quickly updated him about her questioning with the police.

'Do you think ...' Kisha said at end, 'the Heartbreak Club killed Ahaan?'

'That's a very serious crime, Kisha. But I don't know. It's difficult to say. Let's not arrive at any conclusions. Let the police do their job.'

'Hmm, you're right.'

They chatted for some more time and then ended the call, calling it a night. Two minutes later, her phone buzzed with a message. Kisha immediately checked it, thinking it must be Tavish. But it was a notification on her school app. She opened it to realise a new chat window had popped up. There were four participants: King, Rook, Knight and Pawn. The fifth one in the group was her. The messages started pouring in:

KING: We got your message.

It was obviously aimed at Kisha but she didn't respond.

KNIGHT: Welcome to the club, our new Bishop. Ahaan has not only been deeply damaged but he has vanished too. Just the kind of thing we love to do.

Kisha tried to screenshot the chat but a warning appeared on the chat window that screenshots were not allowed.

ROOK: Nor will screen recording work. So don't waste your time, Bishop.

Kisha frowned, realising she was the one being addressed as Bishop. She responded and noticed her chat name appeared as BISHOP.

BISHOP: I had nothing to do with Ahaan's disappearance.

KING: We are giving you one more chance to join us. Make a video where you confess your involvement in Ahaan's disappearance. And you will officially be a member of the Heartbreak Club.

Kisha wondered why they were extending this extra chance to her. It occurred to her that THC's back was really against the wall. Just like hers was, in a way. The point was, who would bow down first in front of the other.

BISHOP: I'm not doing anything of that sort.

No message came for some time.

KING: Alright. You just compromised your only chance to know what happened to your elder sister. Such a pity.

Even before Kisha could message anything else, the others left the chat.

The only one left in the room was Bishop. Kisha Sen felt like a fool.

TWENTY-FOUR

KISHA FELT SHE WAS RIGHT ON THE EMOTIONAL EDGE. Since the last few days, she had found herself oscillating between decisions, choices and pursuits. Every time she made a decision between pursuing Anara's disappearance or letting it go, something new came up to make her reconsider. It was true that she had come to Fairmont High to find out more about her sister's disappearance, but her budding relationship with Tavish was also important to her. Her heart wanted her to focus on it, but circumstances kept pulling her in a different direction. First it was Ahaan's abrupt disappearance and now the Heartbreak Club's new proposal.

When Kisha had left the message for the club, she had thought it would put them on the back foot and they would tell her what had happened to Ahaan. She didn't think they would renegotiate and put her in a spot. It was their offense. Dangling the carrot of information about her sister's disappearance. But what they were asking in return was something which could jeopardise her studies, her future, her career, her life, her everything. Maybe that's what they wanted. To take her confessional video and then not let her join, and use it as leverage against her. Once they had the video, they could blackmail her into giving up looking for Anara as well as Ahaan. As she stood by the window of her room, looking out into the blank, dark sky, Kisha wondered what options she had.

When she reached the academic building the next morning, the first thing she did was meet Tavish. The two of them went to the café. When they entered there was only one student, a girl, sitting and drinking her smoothie. Kisha and Tavish settled into a corner table. With a deep breath, Kisha told Tavish about the previous night's chat and THC's new demand. He remained lost in thought for some time.

'Will you please say something?' She nudged him feeling restless.

'I'm just thinking, what if you actually give them what they want? Then you will get into the club.'

'There's no guarantee they'll keep their word and include me. Maybe the chat was just a trap. Once they get me on video, confessing, there's no way I can exert any kind of pressure on them. Even if I discover concrete proof of their involvement.'

'You have a point, but I have a solution,' Tavish said. Kisha looked at him with a mix of curiosity and hope.

'You make the confessional video, where you admit to being involved in Ahaan's disappearance. But once your "confession" ends, you turn the camera towards me and I become your witness and speak on camera to say that a false confession has been coerced out of you, as an initiation challenge to get into the Heartbreak Club. I make it clear that your so-called confession is not real but a ploy by the club.'

Kisha looked at Tavish sceptically. He read her thoughts and said, 'Hear me out. You only send THC an edited video which just has your confession. We keep the entire video, with my footage, under wraps for our safety. We use it later for leverage and to protect you.'

They heard the assembly bell. Both headed towards the morning assembly, Kisha still thinking about what Tavish had said. By the end of the assembly, Kisha had decided to go with Tavish's plan. It was the best solution in sight. She could get what she wanted out of the club and still keep herself safe. Kisha couldn't thank Tavish enough for coming up with the plan.

Once she'd made up her mind, Kisha waited for the classes to get over so she could record the video with Tavish. But a constant restlessness made her excuse herself during the first class of the day and message Tavish to join her beside the cooler. When Tavish reached there, Kisha told him she was planning to record the video and send it in the next minute.

'Now?' he asked. He had thought she would record it after the classes were over for the day. Kisha nodded. He knew her mind was made up, so he asked her to get on with it.

Kisha switched the camera of her phone and tapped on the video mode. As the recording started, Kisha started speaking slowly, looking at herself in the camera, feeling her heart beat harder with every passing second.

'Hi there. I don't know whom to address this to exactly, but let me get to the point. I am Kisha Sen, a student of Fairmont High, currently studying in India. And I'm making this video in all my senses, without any pressure or influence, to confess that I did try and woo Ahaan Rawat for the last couple of months. As an outcome of my actions, he fell in love with me. But I broke his heart, which damaged him so much that it has played a role in his sudden disappearance from the school. Even though I may be responsible for it, I hope he is fine wherever he is.' Kisha let go off a deep breath.

Her eyes went to the timer. It was already forty-five-second long. Two seconds later, she gently turned the camera towards Tavish. As they'd decided, he now spoke on the camera, 'Kisha is recording this video because she has been asked to do so by the Heartbreak Club, who we think is responsible for not only Ahaan's disappearance but Kisha's elder sister, Anara's as well.' Kisha showed a thumbs up after which she ended the video.

'Thank you so much for this, Tavish,' Kisha said.

He gave her a quick hug, and said, 'I've to go now,' Tavish ran to join his class. Kisha too scooted to her own classroom. Sitting there, she edited the video and sent it to Tavish. He sent her a couple of thumbs-up emojis after which she relaxed. During the break between classes, she ran to the library and repeated what she had done the day before with a pink marker this time, and the same book. The words she highlighted were, of course, different.

MADE. THE. CONFESSION. VIDEO. HOW. DO. I. SEND. IT.

She hoped after what happened in the chatroom, they would still accept her video. Her heart said they would. For a moment, Kisha thought of just waiting in the library to see who would come and pick up the book. But then she realised THC members wouldn't be stupid to come to the library when she was in or even around it. They knew her, but she didn't know them at all. And it could be anybody. Probably someone she passed by, while coming to the library or someone she glanced at in the washroom or met during the assembly. It dawned on her that there was also a chance that the members could also be people she knew. Like Ahaan. The thought scared her.

That night, while having her dinner, Kisha got a call from Tavish.

'I heard that the police has sealed Ahaan's room and seized all of his belongings,' she heard him say. Whenever Tavish jumped directly to the point on a call, she knew it was something serious.

'Okay and?' she asked.

'The only thing they didn't get is his mobile phone.'

'So that means his phone is with him,' Kisha said.

'Here's the catch. The police checked, and his phone is not only switched off but the last network tower it caught was the one nearest to our school.'

'Is their discovery suggesting that the phone is on the school campus?'

'Something like that. I hope it's not with you.'

'No. Why would I have Ahaan's phone?'

'I know it's absurd but I just thought of checking.'

'Okay, but obviously I have no idea where his phone is, so you can relax,' Kisha said. They spoke till her dinner was over. She ended the call and went back to her room. She noticed the block beside her room was red. Every room in the hostel had a wooden block beside the main door outside. When it lit up red, it meant there was some postal mail which the student had to collect from the hostel's reception. Kisha went downstairs. The same receptionist was sitting there, the one with the perennially disinterested face. Kisha always felt bad for her, considering how monotonous her job was.

'Hi, I've a red signal by the door.'

'Name?' The receptionist asked nonchalantly.

'Kisha Sen.'

The receptionist turned towards a box kept beside her, looked through some mail and a few parcels and finally found one with Kisha's name on it. Kisha took it, thanked her and turned to leave. As she took the stairs to reach her floor, Kisha first pressed the A6 size paper envelope. It seemed to have some document inside it. She looked at her name on it. Her parents weren't supposed to send her anything. And if they did, they would have told her to expect it. Or her father could have simply hand delivered it to her.

Wondering who it could be from, she checked the sender's address and name written on the left side of the bottom of the parcel. Her heart leapt into her mouth. She stopped in her tracks and re-read the name. The sender's address was Fairmont High International School, Noida, while the sender's name was: A. Sen.

Anara Sen, Kisha thought. Her throat had gone bone-dry by then.

TWENTY-FIVE

KISHA STARED AT THE ENVELOPE BLANKLY FOR A SECOND. Then, as another girl passed her by, on the stairs, she snapped back to her senses. She ran up to her room, closed the main door and, without wasting a second, tore open the parcel. What tumbled out didn't make sense to begin with. Why would someone send her a reversible sketch in Anara's name? And as soon as she registered the reversible sketch, Kisha knew who would have sent it. Ahaan Rawat. She turned the image upside down and noticed it was of a girl's face. She squinted hard at it, unable to recall where she had seen the very familiar looking face. When she realised who it was, Kisha sat down on her study chair with a thud, joining all the dots together.

Ahaan had said he would prove he was the Bishop in a day's time. Was this his way of doing that? And Anara's name was simply so he wouldn't have to use his own name, but also a way of determining that Kisha opened the envelope. Maybe the person whose sketch it was had a connection to Anara's disappearance? Kisha had a lot of questions but the most important of them all, at the moment, was why was Selena's face on the reversible sketch? The only thing Kisha could conclude was that Selena had a role to play in Anara's disappearance, beyond what she had told Kisha.

Kisha called up Tavish and relayed to him all that had

happened. He was quiet. She knew he was thinking through everything and trying to get to the next step. Kisha adored this about Tavish. He was always about solution rather than panic. In the few seconds of silence that followed, she too was worrying about what to do next?

'I think I should inform the police about this,' she blurted what was on her mind.

'I was thinking the same thing. But if the police get an inkling of this courier, they would invariably rope you in. Like, why did Ahaan send you this? Why in Anara's name? You'll have to tell the truth. Are you willing to talk about everything?'

Tavish was right. Kisha thought hard and suddenly spoke up with excitement.

'What if I inform the police about the parcel but don't give them the correct reversible sketch?'

'What would we gain from that?'

'One, the police's investigation will be in the right direction. They will be able to find out when and from where the courier was sent. That would help us confirm if it was indeed Ahaan who sent it. I mean the sketch is of Ahaan's but we have to be sure if it's him who sent it.'

'Okay and?'

'And it won't put Selena on the police's radar just yet because I would show them this envelope but not this sketch.'

'But why do you want to protect Selena?'

'Not protect. I want to find out myself first how Selena is involved in all this. I want to know if this sketch is hinting towards something genuine or it's another trap for me, laid by the club. If this is indeed Ahaan's idea of proving to me that he is the Bishop, then what does it mean?' *All I know right now is Selena was Anara's girlfriend, but why send her sketch.* Kisha thought.

'Okay ... what do you have in mind?' Tavish asked.

'I am not sure yet. It's something vague ... something still taking shape.' When Kisha ended the call, she told herself that the rest of the puzzle would come together once she knew how exactly Selena fitted in. Her hunch was Ahaan, in all probability, hadn't disappeared on his own.

Kisha put her plan into action immediately. She took one of the many reversible sketches Ahaan had given her, put it in the half-torn envelope and took it to the principal's office.

Dr Iyer called the police the moment Kisha submitted the envelope to him. The officer was in the school before even the first class had started.

As she had expected, Kisha was called to the principal's office, where she saw Officer Pallavi waiting for her.

'Thanks for sharing this information with us, Kisha. It's very helpful.'

'Of course. Ahaan is a friend. It was my duty.'

'Would you like to tell us why you think it was Ahaan? On the envelope, the sender's name is A. Sen.'

'I don't know why the envelope says that, honestly. But I thought it was Ahaan because he used to gift me these reversible sketches. I've more in my room.'

'I think I'll need to see all of them.'

All of them except one, Kisha thought and said, 'Sure. Should I get them now?'

Kisha went to her room and came back with the sketches in fifteen minutes.

'Thank you, Kisha. We'll keep these. In case something

comes up, I may have to call you again,' Officer Pallavi said, getting up and collecting the sketches.

'Sure, ma'am.'

While Kisha headed to her class, her partner was already tracking Selena closely. Kisha had spoken to Jas during breakfast and enlisted her help. Jas had readily agreed; she was always up for a good adventure.

Jas followed Selena during the day. Kisha had asked her to trail Selena around and record her if anything looked fishy. She was also to maintain a record of who all Selena met through the day. When Jas met Kisha during dinner, she told her whatever she had seen and observed through the day. But nothing was useful. They repeated the same drill for four days. Neither Selena was showing any sign of her connection to the Heartbreak Club or Anara, nor was the club responding to her video confession. There was fear lurking within. What if the club's King meant it when the person said she had lost the opportunity to be a club member? Would they really not reconsider it? Kisha knew only time would tell. But how much time?

The only new information came in on the fifth day, from Officer Pallavi who told the principal, who in turn informed Kisha, that it was indeed Ahaan who had couriered her the sketch. Officer Pallavi had tracked the envelope back to the courier company and gone through their CCTV footage. She had spotted Ahaan coming in with the envelope. Only, the footage was from the evening before he disappeared. The courier would have been delivered the next day, but apparently Ahaan had requested it be delivered a day later.

'Do you have any idea why he would do that?' Dr Iyer asked Kisha.

Kisha shook her head but wondered if it was perhaps because he had told her he would prove to her in a day that he was the Bishop. When she met Tavish later in the day, she told him about what the principal had said about Ahaan.

'So, Selena has to be involved somehow. It can't be random that Ahaan made it a point to send you her sketch.'

'We will know soon,' Kisha murmured.

On the sixth day, when Jas told Kisha nothing unusual had happened even on that day, Kisha knew she had to change her approach. She thought deep and hard. She couldn't reach out to the Heartbreak Club. She had to understand Selena's role first. She started thinking about all that had happened in school since her arrival. The last big thing that struck her was how THC had included her as their Bishop in a chat. Would Selena's phone lead to something? Kisha didn't even ask herself twice. She immediately called Jas.

'Jas, I need you to flick Selena's phone. I can't do it because Selena, if she is indeed part of THC, would easily guess it's me who must have pulled this off.'

Jas thought about it for some time and then said, 'Okay, I'll do it. But if I'm caught, I'll have to take your name.'

'Of course,' Kisha said.

Jas got her chance when Selena went to the swimming club. As she entered the changing room, Jas casually entered too. Selena didn't seem to notice Jas at all. In fact, that was one of the reasons Kisha had chosen Jas to shadow Selena. Jas was someone who got along with everyone and was seen all over the campus. She was such a familiar sight, that nobody thought much of her presence anywhere, even if she was somewhere she shouldn't be.

In a stroke of luck for Jas, Selena ran into a friend. While she was chatting with her, Jas switched on her camera and placed it carefully on a shelf, opposite Selena's locker. Selena walked up to her locker, punched in her code to put her stuff inside. Once she was done, Selena locked her locker and headed towards the changing room.

There were three other girls near the lockers and Jas hoped they would leave before Selena came out of the changing room, but her prayers weren't answered. Selena was out in a flash before the other girls could leave. Jas' heart was racing. She turned towards the lockers to avoid any eye contact with Selena. From the corner of her eyes, she saw Selena head to the pool. As she dived for a swim, Jas scampered back to Selena's locker. She quickly checked the video on her phone, and punched the numbers. The locker opened. Jas took Selena's phone which was lying in there, shut the locker and quickly moved out of there.

Jas went to the café, looking for Kisha. She saw her sitting by herself and reading. She walked up to her and discreetly kept Selena's phone on her table. 'Just be careful. I hope the "locate-my-phone" feature is turned off,' she said and slipped away.

Kisha knew what she meant. She would have to be careful. She stared at the phone for some time and then touched it. The screen lit up asking for a password. Kisha had hoped against hope that there wouldn't be a password, though she knew it was unlikely. She threw her head back in exasperation, wondering what she would do now. And if Jas was right and the 'locate-my-phone' feature was actually on, she'd be in deep trouble.

TWENTY-SIX

KISHA CAME BACK TO HER ROOM, SULKING. HER WHOLE plan had fallen flat. The risk she had made Jas take, when she stole Selena's phone, had turned out to be useless because the phone couldn't be unlocked. She was very frustrated. When Jas saw her during dinner, she came up to her and said, 'So? Was the purpose solved?'

Kisha looked up at her, dismayed. 'The phone is locked.'

'Oh damn. Now what? Did you try to hack it? You've got to be quick. Selena has lodged a complaint with the lost and found department of the school. I'm sure the longer the phone is with you, the higher the risk. 'But then again, if she hasn't found the phone yet that means the "locate-my-phone" feature is not on,' Jas concluded.

'It doesn't matter. I don't know the pass code and I have no idea how we can hack the phone—'

'Wait a minute,' Jas said as if struck by an idea. She took Selena's phone from Kisha and typed the same number she had seen her put in for her swimming room locker. Kisha noticed a Cheshire cat like smile spread on Jas' face as she gave the phone back to Kisha. It was unlocked.

'How on earth did you do that?' Kisha couldn't hide her surprise. She realised her voice sounded unusually high pitched.

'Magic!' Jas said with an amused face. 'Now don't waste time. Go and do what you need to.'

Kisha gave her a quick hug, left her dinner mid-way, and went straight to her room. She felt a little guilty about lying to Jas. She'd told her that she suspected Selena of having some sort of a secret affair with Tavish and hence she needed to check her phone. To assuage her guilt, Kisha told herself that the less Jas knew, the better it was for her. And of course, the lie meant Jas had no further questions about the phone.

Kisha started browsing Selena's phone. From her photo gallery to WhatsApp chats to her social media DMs—she scanned everything. Kisha wasn't sure what she was looking for, but she hoped something in there would give her a clue as to why Ahaan had sent her Selena's sketch.

After two hours of searching, Kisha gave up in exasperation. She hurled both her and Selena's phones on the bed and started thinking of other ways through which she could find out more about Selena's involvement. She picked up her phone to call Jas and tell her to take Selena's phone away and put it somewhere it could be found easily by her or the lost & found people, when she noticed her own phone's notification. The same notification came on Selena's phone too.

As Kisha tapped on her notification, she noticed a chat room had been formed in the school app. The same would have happened on Selena's phone too? Kisha felt a knot in her stomach. She was perhaps one step away from knowing something important. Instantly, she appeared in the chat room with the username 'Bishop'. The first message appeared in no time. Kisha was about to enter through Selena's phone as well but she held back her fingers at the nick of time. King had already messaged in the chat room.

KING: Rook's phone has been stolen.

Letting out short-hot breaths, Kisha registered two things: one, Selena was Rook. Confirmed. Two, the fact that they included her as Bishop, still, meant they would consider her video recording.

KNIGHT: Share the video here, Bishop.

Kisha did as asked. She shared the edited video with the group. Nobody messaged till it loaded. Once done, King saved and then deleted the video from the chat room.

KING: No further meeting till Rook's phone is found or Rook logs in from another phone after her identity validation. Out … everyone.

Kisha's hands were shaking. She finally understood why Ahaan had sent Selena's sketch. He was giving her his proof of being the Bishop by exposing the identity of another member of the group. Selena was the Rook. Now there were just four more identities left to be unmasked: Pawn, Knight, Queen and of course, the King. How would she discover them? The idea struck instantly. Ahaan's way would take her forward. The following day was Sunday. Kisha went to various courier shops till she found one that didn't have a CCTV, and couriered a single note in Selena's name.

Selena was surprised to receive an envelope in the courier, the next day. She opened it, uncertain of what to expect. She wondered if this could be a lead to her missing phone. As she read the words on the page, her heart started palpitating hard.

'I know you are the Rook. Write the names of the other members behind this note and leave it in your swimming club locker. Don't try to change the pass code or any other tricks. You have one day or I expose you to the police.' Selena's heart was racing. The two words which made her panic were *expose* and *police*.

Selena Alvi turned to catch her reflection in the mirror of her room. She had been studying in Fairmont High International, since the first standard. That meant eleven years of her life. And she'd heard about the Heartbreak Club for the first time when she was in the second standard. Fairmont High's canteen only had vegetarian food, and yet, one day, someone had mixed non-veg food with it, causing a storm in the canteen. There was a big hoopla about it, but nobody was caught. Everyone said perhaps the Heartbreak Club was behind it. Little Selena had been impressed with the daredevilry and the seed for her innate obsession with the club had been sown.

Her interest in the club continued as the years progressed. From various sources over the years, Selena learnt more about the club and whatever she pieced together fascinated her. They had come to be known as people who would force failures on students whose heart was set on something, be it a person or a goal.

Her dream of being a part of the club was realised when, one day, the club reached out to her with a proposal for their dreaded black handshake. She couldn't believe her luck that the club she had been in awe of, a club that had attained a mythical status within the school campus, had given her a chance to be a part of it.

Selena was given her target, a junior named Vaibhav. She had to make Vaibhav fall in love with her and break his heart in a way that left him deeply damaged. Selena not only accomplished the task, but was surprised at how much she enjoyed it. Especially the way the thrill to join the Heartbreak Club made her explore her own dark side. It took her five weeks to complete the task. And the best part of it was she did it all online, merely by chatting with Vaibhav. She toyed with him emotionally, got him completely involved and then she simply ghosted him.

By the time she disappeared from what was a completely digital relationship, catfishing to be precise, Vaibhav was near a nervous breakdown. He had to leave school and focus on his mental health. Not only was Selena successfully inducted as the Rook in the club but she realised what the principal role of each member was. In total, there were six members at any given point of time in the club. Their roles were clearly demarcated:

King: the role of the King was to lead the group, plan the next 'thing' in school and also spot the subsequent King for the club. He was the torchbearer of the club and on him rested the future of the club. His decision on anything couldn't be superseded.

Queen: the Queen was the second in command. Her role was to execute whatever the King decided.

Knight: the role of the Knight, along with the Bishop, was to be on the lookout for the next student whose heart had to be broken.

Bishop: the Bishop was the one who physically carried out whatever the Knight and Bishop decided, as far as communicating with a potential target was concerned.

Rook: the Rook was the doorkeeper of the club. No

outsider could get in touch with the club without the Rook's approval. The role of the Rook was to mislead people. If someone was being too nosy and trying to find out about the club, be it any student or teacher or even the principal, the Rook would step in and lead them astray. Selena had tried to mislead Kisha by informing her that she was Anara's girlfriend. And it was her who had orchestrated the attack on her to scare her away.

Pawn: the role of the Pawn was to physically carry out certain activities that the club demanded. The errand runner to be precise.

The ultimate attraction, to join and be in the club, was that the members would be amongst the top students passing out of the school. THC always leaked the final examination paper to its members. And the master stroke of the club was that only the King knew all the other members by face. The rest didn't know who all were in the club. This development, Selena was told, had happened with the advancement in the digital communication in the last five years. Though, in Kisha's case, this was broken since everyone else knew Kisha was the new Bishop. But then they had different plans for her.

Being a part of the club had been a high for Selena. Seeing people getting affected by the club's actions, and yet get away without consequences, was a thrill that she hadn't known she would enjoy so much. The club made her feel cool, confident and rebellious. But she felt the opposite of all those things now, as she stood in her room, staring at her reflection, clutching the note couriered to her. Who could it be who'd discovered her identity? And how? Her missing phone had to be a part of it, she was sure.

Not only was she scared of what the school authorities or the police might do to her, she was also scared of the club. The club took its secrecy very seriously. She feared she could be the first member whose identity had been exposed. And she knew the punishment well. If any of the members got to know her anonymity had been compromised—willingly or otherwise—her video would be out. The video where she'd confessed to having manipulated Vaibhav. The Heartbreak Club kept the black handshake videos as leverage against the members. Only the King had access to the videos. Selena picked up a pen, tore a blank sheet of paper from a notebook and sat down to write on it.

Kisha had seen Selena take the courier from the reception. And she couldn't stay calm. She was waiting for her to come and head towards the swimming club. Something told her that there was no way Selena would try to fight it. She had to agree to obey what was written in the note.

The moment she had been waiting for arrived before dinner. Selena went down towards the swimming club. Kisha called Jas. As per their plan, Jas reached the locker room before Selena arrived there. Selena entered, put the page inside her locker and locked it. As she moved out, Jas too moved behind her. She had her ear piece on, where she was on a call with Kisha. It was important for them to keep Selena under observation. Basic sense said she wouldn't be informing THC about the note. And if she did, Kisha, the new Bishop, would anyway find out.

Seeing Selena return to the girls' hostel, Kisha rushed to the swimming club. There was nobody there at the time she reached. She quickly went to the locker and unlocked it with the same pass code Jas had given her. Kisha took out the page. Taking a deep breath, she began to read.

Her first thoughts were Selena had lied through her teeth.

TWENTY-SEVEN

'THOUGH IT'S TRUE THAT I'M THE ROOK BUT I DON'T KNOW anyone else in the club. Nobody does except the King. Please believe me. If my name comes out, my life and career will be ruined. Hope you understand.'

Kisha read and re-read the note several times sitting in her room. Selena had to be lying. If nobody, but the king, knew the identity of the members, then how did Ahaan know that Selena was the Rook? Kisha also realised that the Heartbreak Club probably had a video of Selena's, just like they had one of Kisha. Something wasn't adding up. And she couldn't trust Selena anymore. She would have to put her through another test.

Kisha went to Jas' room. She needed help and knew that if she wanted Jas to help her, she had to come clean about what was going on. No excuses would work and Kisha didn't want to lie to her and put doubts in her mind.

'Damn. I never thought I would ever unmask a Heartbreak Club member. This is exciting. Did you tell Tavish?' Jas was incredulous when she heard everything.

Kisha shook her head. She had not told Tavish about the Selena ordeal. In fact, though she had told Jas the rest of it, she had not yet told her that she was now the Bishop instead of Ahaan.

'Why not?' Jas asked.

'Selena is Tavish's batchmate. If I tell Tavish, he'll feel compelled to come up with some solution. But I'm sure he'll want to get involved but that could warn Selena. And any odd behavior from him may be noted by her. I can't risk that. Not at this stage. That's why even I didn't follow her myself all these days. I asked you to.'

'I get it but everything is a risk in that sense. Tell me, why trust me? For all you know, even I could be a member. Have you thought about it?' Jas asked, her inherently mischievous eyes narrowing.

Well, even I'm a member, Kisha thought and said, 'If you are, you are the only one I've got. I can't go to Vega for this.'

Jas laughed.

'Now listen,' Kisha said, 'we have to get the truth out of Selena. The good thing is she doesn't know that it's us who know her identity.'

'What do you have in mind?'

'Nothing. That's why I wanted to discuss it with you.'

The two brainstormed for a long while and finally arrived at a plan. According to Jas, who knew everything about everyone, Selena couldn't handle alcohol one bit, but was always the first one to indulge. Kisha and Jas decided they would secretly arrange a girls' drinking night in the hostel and invite a few select girls. One of them would be Selena.

Jas spoke to her friends in the boys' hostel and smuggled some alcohol to the girls' hostel, the following day. She invited Kisha, as per plan, Selena, and some of her friends to her room. As the drinking session happened, Kisha made sure she was close to Selena. She waited patiently for a hook to bait her towards the conversation she wanted to have. When she saw

Selena had had quite a few drinks and was now slurring, Kisha started by mentioning Anara.

'You know, you were Anara di's girlfriend and yet I know so little about you. When did Anara di come out to you as a lesbian? Did she propose first?' Kisha asked, wanting to ease Selena into the conversation.

Selena glanced at Kisha. She seemed to be having difficulty focusing. Kisha knew that Selena may be aware that she was the new Bishop. But that wasn't the point. She hoped alcohol superseded her senses at that moment.

'Lesbian?' Selena laughed. 'Anara wasn't a lesbian. C'mon.'

So, it was a lie, Kisha thought. She waited for Selena to reveal more. Kisha knew by then that Selena was completely under the influence of alcohol.

'Anara was bi. She did have a boyfriend at one point but then she broke up. After that she had a girlfriend.'

Kisha frowned. If Anara being a lesbian was news to her, her being bi was not any less of a surprise.

'You say she had a girlfriend. But that was you, right? Anara di's girlfriend?' It was a question framed to trick her.

'Naw! It wasn't me. I'm completely straight.'

'Then?'

'Both are my batchmates.'

'Is it? Who are they?'

Selena didn't talk immediately. She poured herself some more tequila from the bottle which she had grasped like a possessive lover, gulped it neat and then slurred, 'Malvika Oberoi.'

Malvika Oberoi, Kisha uttered the name under her breath, hearing it for the first time. 'But I never heard of or met anyone by that name from your batch,' she said. *And if this girl was really close to Anara, then at least Tavish would have told her about it*, Kisha thought.

Selena didn't hear Kisha. In her drunken state she looked at Kisha and said, 'And the boyfriend … it's Tavish Mathur.'

TWENTY-EIGHT

SELENA WAS GOING ON BLABBERING BUT KISHA COULDN'T hear a word. Her mind was totally blank. And by the time she realised she should push Selena to know more, the latter had passed out. Selena was made to sleep in Jas room while the others, including Kisha, went back to their respective rooms once the alcohol was over. They dispersed one by one so they weren't caught.

In her own bed, Kisha was wide awake. The information Selena had given her, was playing on her mind. Tavish was Anara's boyfriend? Why had he never mentioned that? Kisha didn't know whether to be angry or weep? She wasn't even sure she could trust Selena's drunken information. But could she trust the boy she loved? Or had she trusted him too easily. The more Kisha tried to pull out an answer from the bowl of questions Selena had triggered in her, the more hopeless she felt. In the end, she decided she would first do what she could—confirm whether Selena had told her the truth. A lot was at stake.

To verify Selena's information, Kisha employed the same method as before. This time she chose to get the envelope in Selena's name, delivered the same day. Selena received the envelope, her hands shaking, read the question and then wrote her answer on the same paper. Then, same as last time, she left the note in her swimming club locker. The question was a tricky one. Kisha had to phrase it in such a way that Selena didn't suspect her. Thus, she couldn't directly mention Anara. When Kisha read Selena's answer she understood what her mother meant when she used to tell her, at times, that her BP was falling. She felt the same. The question Kisha had asked was: *Are the two disappearances from school related? Did they have any romantic partners?*

Kisha hoped this question was general enough, something even the police could've asked. It didn't give Selena cause to think it could be Kisha in particular. It somehow projected that the one who wrote the question perhaps wasn't close to either of the two students who disappeared, hence no names were mentioned.

Selena's answer was: *I don't know about Ahaan much. Kisha was asked to woo her as part of her black handshake but THC knew she wouldn't be able to pass because of the inherent twistedness of it and it would end her pursuance of the club members. And even if she did pass, THC would have given her wrong information about Anara, to convince Kisha that the club wasn't responsible for Anara's disappearance. All I know about Anara is that she was exploring her sexuality. Her boyfriend was Tavish, though she never made it public, while her girlfriend was Malvika Oberoi. She is in the UK now as part of the student exchange program. I seriously don't know beyond this. I beg you not to reach out to me. If THC comes to know that my anonymity has been compromised or that I've given you this information, my life will be destroyed. Please understand.*

Selena's fear was almost palpable. That these messages

caused her dread, was obvious. But that wasn't something Kisha cared about at the moment. Selena had not been lying. She had repeated, in her senses, what she'd said when drunk. Also, the part about Kisha wooing Ahaan was correct too. Kisha had decided that if what Selena had said, turned out to be true, she would confront Tavish. There was no looking back now.

Kisha called Tavish and asked him to meet her at the rugby field. It would be empty in the evening, since the closing time of the field was 6 p.m.

'All okay?' Tavish asked, joining her. He'd noted she sounded edgy on the call.

Kisha plunged right into it. 'Why did you hide the fact that Anara di and you were dating?'

The question may be straightforward, but there were too many feelings hidden in it. The most prominent of them was hurt. Tavish knew she had seen through him, in that moment, and that he couldn't lie to her anymore. *Should he apologise or explain*, he wondered.

'Look Kisha, you've to know what was between Anara and me was—'

'Tell me. I want to know.'

'Anara and I were in a relationship for a month. It was more from my end then hers, still we were in a relationship, none the less. But that was also the time when she told me that she couldn't be with me as she ...'

'As she what?'

'She was in love with a girl.'

'Malvika Oberoi.'

'How do you know?' Tavish's surprise was genuine.

'First tell me, why didn't you tell me all this before?'

'I thought it wasn't necessary. With Anara, it was more of an infatuation. With you, it was love. And I didn't want to cloud your perception of me. I mean I was sure if I'd told you, *we* wouldn't have happened.'

Kisha couldn't deny that. If she knew Tavish had dated her elder sister—infatuation or whatever—she would have checked her feelings for him.

'But do you have any idea what this means for our relationship, now that I've discovered all this from someone else? If you don't have any idea then let me tell you. You've lost my trust.'

'Who told you?'

'That's not the point, Tavish. The point is how do I build my trust in you again? How?'

Kisha stomped her foot on the ground, frustrated, and turned to walk away. Tavish wanted to stop her but knew this wasn't the time. He watched her disappear towards the girls' hostel lane. Then he let out a scream, hoping it would make him feel better. It didn't.

Kisha walked into her next class, only to be asked by the teacher to proceed to the library. The police were there and wanted to talk to her. As she was about to enter the library, she noticed Vega leaving. She looked at Kisha, came close and said, 'I'm sorry. I had to because I was pressurised.'

Vega walked away, leaving a confused Kisha. She entered the library and noticed Officer Pallavi and Dr Juneja there. Nobody else seemed to be around. Kisha went and stood before them. The way Officer Pallavi looked at her, Kisha knew something was amiss. The warmth she had felt last time was missing.

'Vega showed us photographic and video evidence that Ahaan and you were dating,' she said and showed Kisha both the photo and the video. It was of the time when he had abruptly kissed her in the library, a video Vega had recorded and shared with Tavish. Kisha knew if she accepted the fact, she would go against what she had told Officer Pallavi before. And if she tried to explain, the police would think she was trying to weave a story.

'Kisha, if there's anything that you want to tell us, then please do so now. Before it's too late.' The first part was comforting. The second was a threat.

'We weren't dating, ma'am. Ahaan told me he had feelings for me but I didn't reciprocate. In the video too, maybe you can see, he had initiated the kiss. I didn't.' Kisha chose to mix a little bit of truth and a little bit of lie to clear her stand.

'What was your reaction to this act of Ahaan's? Did you report it to your parents or teachers?'

'No. I just warned him not to repeat it. And he didn't. If he had I would have reported it.'

'And you still don't know what happened to Ahaan?'

'If I did, I would have definitely told you, ma'am.'

Officer Pallavi knew Kisha was a minor and a student. She could only put pressure on her to a certain extent. She let her go. Kisha walked out, relieved, knowing there were chances she could be summoned again. She thought of asking Vega why she had shown the video to them, knowing it was misleading, but she didn't. She had more important things to do. Like, get to Malvika Oberoi.

That night, a person in a dark hoodie, went to the under-construction swimming pool site, within the school campus, at the dead of night. The person checked the spots where the bodies of Anara and then Ahaan had been buried. Everything seemed the same, undiscovered. Relieved, the person then walked away diffusing into the darkness around.

Meanwhile, Kisha figured out the names of the five students who had gone to the London branch of Fairmont High, when Kisha and four others had come to the Noida branch. The names were: Malvika Oberoi, Vedan Shah, Daksh Malhotra, Zica Sharma and Nivit Basu.

Kisha tried to get Malvika's number from the same teacher who coordinated the student exchange program, and who had given her all the five names, but the teacher refused and asked her to get the principal's consent. Kisha, instead, searched for Malvika's social media profile, added her and DM-ed her.

Hi,

This is Anara's sister. I need to talk urgently. Could you please let me know your phone number?

Thanks xo.

She waited but no response came that night. When Kisha was having breakfast in the canteen, the morning after, she noticed a message notification. Malvika had finally responded.

Hey Kisha,

I know who you are. The anonymous message about THC's involvement in Anara's disappearance was sent by me. Here's my phone number. Call me anytime.

Cheers.

Kisha frowned reading the message. So Malvika was the one who had messaged her. It was mostly due to that message that Kisha had opted for the student exchange program and decided to be here. Kisha immediately saved her number and called Malvika on Facetime.

'Hi Kisha, I was expecting your call,' Malvika said. Her voice was warm and reassuring.

'Was it really you?' Kisha asked, coming straight to the point.

'Yes. I loved Anara but I didn't have the courage to talk to the police. If I blamed the Heartbreak Club, the investigation would surely reveal that Anara and I were a couple and I wasn't ready to come out yet. So I did the next best thing and informed you. I hope you understand.'

'I do.'

'The fact that you have reached me, tells me you must have broken up the club.'

'Not really. I am still trying. Do you know anything else about Anara or the club?'

There was a pause. A weighted pause.

'The King is amongst the ones who came with me to London.'

'What? How do you know?'

'As much as you are trying to figure out what happened

to your sister, I am doing the same. Your sister was the love of my life.'

Kisha could feel a chill run through her spine. The call ended with Malvika telling Kisha she would update her if she discovered more. There were three weeks left for the five students to come back. But it also meant, it would be time for Kisha to go back to Fairmont High International, London. Kisha felt like crying, foreseeing a complete dead end.

Malvika ended her call with Kisha and called the person who had asked her to share her number with Kisha immediately.

'I told Kisha what you asked me to, Tiger,' Malvika said.

'Don't take that name,' Tavish said from the other side of the phone.

'Why? Reminds you of someone?'

'Shut up. I'll talk to you later.' Tavish ended the call and went ahead to join his team mates. He had a rugby match, even though he knew his mind was somewhere else. He had genuinely fallen for Kisha Sen but his love for her wasn't simple. It was black. It was dark. It was complicated. But it was love, nonetheless.

THE HEARTBREAK CLUB: CHAT FILES – 3

THE CHATROOM THAT APPEARED HAD ALL THE CLUB members logging in, except the Bishop and the Queen.

KING: Good you got your phone, Rook. All okay?

ROOK: Yes, King.

KNIGHT: Am I allowed to know where the Queen is?

KING: The Queen isn't well. The person will join us soon. We are here because I wanted to tell you all that for the first time, other members also know about the identity of the Bishop. If I get a whiff that anyone else, except the members, know who the Bishop is, I'll have to take steps which you all may not like. Remember, Kisha Sen is an aberration to the rule. I'll deal with her.

PAWN: Any plan for that, King?

KING: I have two options for Kisha Sen. Depends what she chooses.

KNIGHT: What are the options?

KING: Pretty basic. Life or Death.

Nobody messaged for a few seconds.

KING: Until next time, let's continue to lie low since the police is still around. Out ... everyone.

King left.
Knight left.
Rook left.
Pawn left.
The chat room dissolved.

To be continued
in

The Heartbreak Club
Book 2: The Destruction

ACKNOWLEDGEMENTS

The Heartbreak Club will always be special for me because, like my protagonist, my journey of writing this book stemmed out of tumultuous personal events. This is the first time I'm penning a high school thriller and I hope the excitement with which I wrote the story gets transferred to the readers as they read and enjoy it.

I would like to extend my heartfelt thanks and gratitude to:

Rukun Kaul, for believing in my work and providing an opportunity for a symbiotic collaboration. Hope to tell many more stories together.

Sanghamitra Biswas, for the valuable inputs during the edit process, bringing the book to its publishable present stage.

My readers, for showing love, appreciation and patience for sixteen years now. You all are my strength. And the much needed source of motivation when lazy days come along.

Friends and family, for being there always, unconditionally.

R, for being my constant through Khichdi and Biryani.

www.ingramcontent.com/pod-product-compliance
Lightning Source LLC
LaVergne TN
LVHW010205070526
838199LV00062B/4503